The Matter of the
VANISHING GREYHOUND

Golden Gate Bridge Disappearing Greyhound Bus Caper

Steve Levi

Master of the Impossible Crime

PUBLICATION CONSULTANTS
WE BELIEVE IN THE POWER OF AUTHORS

PO Box 221974 Anchorage, Alaska 99522-1974
books@publicationconsultants.com—www.publicationconsultants.com

ISBN 978-1-59433-651-5
ebook ISBN 978-1-59433-652-2
Library of Congress Catalog Card Number: 2016946816

Copyright 2016 Steve Levi
—First Edition—

All rights reserved, including the right of reproduction in any form, or by any mechanical or electronic means including photocopying or recording, or by any information storage or retrieval system, in whole or in part in any form, and in any case not without the written permission of the author and publisher.

This is a work of fiction. Names, characters, businesses, places, events and incidents are either the products of the author's imagination or used in a fictitious manner. Any resemblance to actual persons, living or dead, or actual events is purely coincidental.

Manufactured in the United States of America.

"There is only one thing in the universe more powerful
than human imagination: human ingenuity."
Detective Heinz Noonan

To remind Michael that nothing is impossible.

Chapter 1

Captain Heinz Noonan, the "Bearded Holmes" of the Sandersonville, North Carolina Police Department, was pleasantly sequestered in the back row of the stretch 737 with a double Cointreau in one hand and Warren Sitka's SOURDOUGH JOURNALIST in the other. Life was going along smoothly until he was tapped on the shoulder by a flight attendant. He quickly covered his plastic glass with the book and looked up innocently.

"Captain Noonan?" the woman asked.

He ignored her, hopeful she would go away.

"Captain Noonan?" She asked again, clearly ignoring the book covered Cointreau.

"Never heard of him," Noonan grumbled as he sank back into the saga of the fossilized alligator of Talkeetna. "He's probably up in First Class." He was re-reading the classic of Alaska, absorbed, and, as he was on his way to Alaska for a two-week vacation, it seemed to make perfect sense to read up on the lore and legends of the Northland. He was also reading the tales so his wife, Alaskan born and proud of it, wouldn't catch him unprepared when they went to Talkeetna for the Moose Dropping Festival – at least that was what she was threatening to do. If there was such a thing as a Moose Dropping Festival. When it came to his wife and her Alaskan friends, as he had discovered over the years, there was no telling when Alaskans were serious or just pulling your leg.

"I'm sure you're mistaken, Captain." This flight attendant was not about to be bamboozled – particularly when she was certain she was correct. "From the description I was given, it's either you, the copilot or the Yuppie in 5B. I was told you could be cantankerous, so that leaves out the Yuppie. He made a pass."

"What about the co-pilot?"

"His beard isn't salt-and-pepper, he isn't hiding out in the back of the airplane, and he doesn't carry a flask of refreshment."

"What makes you think I've brought liquor on board?" Noonan gave her a look of absolute innocence in spite of the fact he had clearly been caught glass-handed, or at least plastic-handed. He had snitched the cup from the plane's galley as he had walked by. He would have liked some ice but he had not been able to find any cubes, so he was living with the indignity of warm liquor.

She gave him the old do-you-think-I-was-born-yesterday look.

"What are you?" he snapped pleasantly. "Some kind of detective?"

"No," she replied with mock pleasantry. "I've got three kids and two of them are teenagers. I'll tell you what I'll do. I'll forget all about the liquor you brought on board if you'll take a walk down to the terminal check-in desk. A man is standing at the counter who's just dying to speak with you."

Noonan stroked his salt-and-pepper beard and looked imploringly into the eyes of the flight attendant. "This is my first vacation in three years. Couldn't you just call the check-in counter and say you couldn't find me? I must have taken another flight, possibly to Denver?"

"Captain Noonan! How am I going to cover myself if you're in the computer for this flight?"

"Lie," he replied dryly. "People do it all the time."

"Not on my watch, Captain. Besides, you're holding up the flight. Why don't you just go down and see what the man wants? I'll hold your seat."

"I know what the man wants," snapped Noonan. "He wants to spoil my vacation."

"Well, tell him," said the flight attendant with a smile, "you need one." Then she reached under the book and took his plastic cup with a finger of Cointreau from his grasp. "I'll hold this for you. We can't have you walking around the terminal with an open container of liquor, can we?"

"Will you hold the plane for me." The question was plaintive.

The flight attendant looked him squarely in the eye. "Do you want me to lie? OK. Sure, I'll hold the flight for you."

She was lying.

The moment Noonan stepped into the passageway leading to the concourse, the door to the Alaska Airlines flight swung shut behind him.

Chapter 1

By the time he made it to the check-in desk at the head of the ramp, he could see the plane and his Alaska vacation disappearing into the labyrinth of approaches at the Seattle-Tacoma International Airport. When he arrived at the courtesy lounge, Flight 132, non-stop to Anchorage, was off the ground.

So was Noonan.

"This had better be an incredible case," he snapped at the Sandersonville Commissioner of Homeland Security Lizzard – a delegate to one of those professional conferences which lasted a day and a half, but you could take a week of vacation since your flight had already been paid for – who was hovering near the complimentary champagne with his hands full of a single glass. Noonan glared down at the bald pate of the Commissioner from the majesty of his 6-foot-2 frame. "I mean, this had better be an incredible story. We'd better be talking about lost mines and hidden treasures, right? Topless dancers and Cointreau by the waterfall? I've paid in advance for a three-day king salmon trip on the Kenai, a flight-seeing trip around Denali and dinner with Warren Sitka." He snarled as he tapped the book he was holding into his open palm. "That's not to mention the heck I'm going to get when I don't arrive in Anchorage and my wife has to explain to her parents and relatives, yet another time, why I'm not coming north – again." He put a heavy accent on the word again.

"Oh, I've taken care of that," Commissioner Lizzard said, stumbling over his words trying to be polite and professional at the same time. "I called Lorelei, and she completely understands. She said she's taken care of the king salmon trip. Your father-in-law will sit in for you."

"What! I pay for the tickets, and my father-in-law takes my place! I've never even been king salmon fishing!"

"Now, now, Captain. It's not all that bad. In fact, I wish I had an assignment like this myself."

"Commissioner Lizzard, don't give me that. What are you doing in Seattle anyway? This is a long way from North Carolina."

"The call of duty, Captain Noonan. The call of duty. I happened to be in Seattle at a conference when the call came. I decided to meet with you myself."

"You're here because everyone else in my office had the good sense not to pull me off a vacation-bound airplane," snapped Noonan. "That's one thing I have to say about my people. They've got the brains to know when not to bother me!"

As Noonan continued to ramble and roar, the Commissioner found himself a chair still conveniently close to the complimentary champagne table and settled in holding his champagne glass in front of him like an offering to the gods. Standing, he barely topped five feet; seated he looked more like a child on a love seat than a man in a recliner. He was so small his black suit appeared like a stain on the massive chair.

Unfortunately for Commissioner Lizzard, just as it appeared Noonan was calming down, a flight attendant appeared with his luggage. The flight attendant recognized Noonan immediately and set the twin suitcases down in front of the detective. Then he did the worst possible thing he could have done under the circumstances. He pulled Noonan's fishing pole tube out from under his left arm and passed it to the detective at the same as he handed him a copy of NOONAN'S LAW, GREATEST CASES F SANDERSONVILLE'S 'BEAREDED HOLMES'

"I'm a great fan," he said as Noonan took the book and fished for a pen. "If you ever get to Alaska, look me up."

Noonan smiled at the attendant, turned slightly, and glared at Commissioner Lizzard. Modestly Noonan signed the book and thanked the attendant for getting the luggage.

"How did you know I was getting off?" Noonan asked suspiciously as he handed the book back to the attendant.

"The Sandersonville Police Department called about an hour ago and asked for your luggage to be pulled off the flight and held. I guess you were already on the plane."

"Apparently." Noonan swiveled his head to the side and shot the Commissioner a look of First Degree Murder.

The flight attendant left without realizing the dynamite stick he had ignited. Noonan looked out the window of the courtesy lounge for a moment, watching the flight line personnel scatter as an Horizon Air flight wallowed toward the terminal. He tapped on the window absentmindedly and then turned back toward the Commissioner who was trying to let the cushions of the recliner suck him to oblivion.

"So you had my luggage taken off the plane? An hour ago?! You let me sit on the plane for half an hour while you debated whether to call me off or not?"

"Well, it's not the way it seems." Commissioner Lizzard was stumbling over his own logic. "The situation was changing with each moment. We weren't sure if you were needed, so we asked to have your bags removed just in case, if you know what I mean."

"No, I don't know what you mean. What I think you are saying is you had my bags taken off, and, should it have come to pass I was not needed, I would have left with my bags here in Seattle while I was on my way to Anchorage."

"No. No. We would have made sure your bags were put on the same flight you were on. It just didn't work out that way."

Noonan watched another Alaska Airlines jet arch into the sky. It was headed north, to the land of king salmon and moose burgers. The sun caught the angles of the plane's metal for a split second, and then it was nothing more than a shining spot in the sky.

"Commissioner," Noonan pointed to the empty sky into which the airplane had just vanished. "I'll have you know three years of waiting and close to $6,000 went north just now. Worse, now I've got to explain to my wife and the twins why I'm not in Alaska with the in-laws when I've been talking about it for years!"

"But I talked with your wife. She said she understood!"

Noonan leaned forward and looked at Commissioner Lizzard over the top of his glasses. "Commissioner. You don't know my wife. That's what she'll tell you. What she'll say to me is going to be quite a bit different. You have no idea what this is going to cost me!"

"No. I promised you would have your vacation right after you dealt with another matter. And you could have three weeks instead of two and the Department will see you are reimbursed for any expenses you can't recover."

Noonan was enraged. "Wake up and smell the ground roast, Commissioner. King salmon season is only open in July. It's what, the 22nd?! Great, I get three weeks' vacation in Alaska when it's illegal to catch king salmon. What a thrill! Did you think this one up all by yourself?"

The Commissioner started to speak, but Noonan continued right over him.

"Who do you think you're fooling by saying the Department is going to pay me back for all my expenses? The Department doesn't have the money to keep the first aid kits in the patrol cars full! Wouldn't I be considered the Department Grinch if I got expense money reimbursement and no one else did?"

Noonan let the question hang while he marched over to the coffee table. He looked for china and had to settle for Styrofoam. Lizzard was silent, waiting for Noonan to fill his cup with decaf.

The Commissioner spoke as if he had an inside angle, which he did. "Actually, it's not our Department that's going to be paying your expenses."

Between bites of the coffee, Noonan snapped, "This had better be good, Commissioner Lizzard. I've been dreaming of barbecued salmon steaks for the past six months."

The Commissioner ignored the Alaska reference and went on as if he had not heard a word the detective has said. "There was another reason to have your luggage pulled. You see, you are going to be taking a trip but, unfortunately for you, it's not to Alaska. You're going south."

"What a thrill. Where am I going?"

"San Francisco. It's another of those Alaska Airlines cities, so we didn't have any trouble getting you booked. First-class this time, what a thrill, eh?"

Noonan was unimpressed. "First class? For a trip lasting, what an hour and a half? How accommodating. And since I'm going to be working, I won't be able to drink. Takes all the fun out of first-class, don't you think?"

Noonan leaned forward aggressively, causing Lizzard to charge on as if he had not heard a word Noonan had spoken. "Well, the San Francisco Police Department said you would have every amenity. That's easy for them to say because they aren't paying the bill. Butterfield-Fargo First National Bank is. That's one of the largest banks in San Francisco, you know. Actually, I believe they're the largest bank chain in California."

"Then it's probably a good bet they're the largest bank chain on the West Coast," snapped Noonan.

"Could be. I don't know." Lizzard said it quickly and then went on so fast Noonan could not get a word in edgewise. "All I know is they're paying your expenses. All of them. All we had to do was agree to lend you to them for the duration of the case."

"Oh, how equitable! I guess that makes me like a shortstop or halfback. I get swapped around. Am I making the same kind of money?"

"Now, Captain, we, er, I understand how you feel. In fact, I'd feel the same way if I had planned on going on vacation, but sometimes things just happen."

"Yeah, don't they?" Noonan was not mollified. "When was the last time you gave up your vacation to go to work for someone else?"

Chapter 1

Lizzard dodged the question. It wasn't a good dodge, but it stopped Noonan from another snippy statement. "All I know at this point, Butterfield-Fargo First National Bank was hit yesterday with a robbery. The thieves got away with about $10 million in cash, who knows how much from the safety deposit boxes and ten hostages."

"What do you mean, 'got away?'" Noonan shook his head as if to clear it. "How can you get away with ten hostages? If the thieves already have the money, what do they need the hostages for?"

"Ah, intrigued already! Fine. Fine. Well, you'll just have to wait until you get to San Francisco to find out. Oh my goodness!" Lizzard looked at his wristwatch in mock astonishment. "It looks as though your flight to San Francisco is boarding now! At Gate B-12! Here! Let me take your bags! Com'on. You don't want to miss your flight! Hurry! Hurry!"

Before Noonan could respond, Lizzard was out of the chair like a cat that's been caught napping where it shouldn't and was hustling Noonan's luggage out the door of the courtesy lounge. Noonan, caught just before he launched into another terse statement, suddenly found himself alone in the courtesy lounge, his fishing pole tube in one hand and a Styrofoam cup of cooling coffee in the other. He shrugged helplessly and set the coffee down. He was about to exit the lounge when he suddenly stopped and glanced into the kitchenette. There he spotted a glass, an actual glass, purloined it, and opened the refrigerator. After he discovered the icebox was empty, he dug four ice cubes out of the champagne bucket and dropped them into his glass. But the professional in him was too strong. Sadly he shook his head and left the glass on the counter.

By the time he got to the boarding area, the Commissioner already had his bags checked in. The Commissioner handed him his ticket. "It's certainly nice of you to be such a good sport, Captain. You don't know how much the Department appreciates this." The Commissioner was all smiles.

"Yeah," snapped Noonan tapping the Commissioner's chest with the end of the fishing pole tube, as aggressive as one can be with one's boss. "Why don't you show your appreciation by taking this back to my office? I don't think I'll be using it in San Francisco." Then he reached inside his jacket and pulled out his flask of Cointreau. "I won't be needing this either. Put it in my desk, away from prying eyes and greedy lips."

"Of course."

"Have my staff go over to my house and send me some of my work clothes. All I have in my suitcases are jeans, work shirts, bug juice and sunglasses. Fortunately, I have my leather jacket with me." He patted his jacket affectionately.

"They're already doing that. We anticipated you wanted your usual work clothes so we're sending them along tomorrow."

"Who am I supposed to meet when I get to San Francisco?" Noonan asked.

"I don't know, but don't worry. I'm sure someone will be there for you when you arrive."

"Oh, goody goody."

* * *

The only nice thing about the trip to San Francisco was that Noonan would be sitting in First Class.

But it was a short trip.

And he could not drink.

And the flight attendant for this flight didn't have half the personality of the one on her way to Alaska. When Noonan finally traipsed down the hallway and entered the First Class cabin, the flight attendant slammed the door behind him and sniped, "Now that we're all here." Then he closed the door to the forward cabin. The plane was moving even before Noonan found his seat belt.

The rest of the passengers didn't seem to mind the delay, at least no one in the First Class rows. On the starboard side of the cabin, two businesswomen in the front row were chatting while behind them, a man wearing sunglasses dressed like a movie producer on holiday was working on a laptop and downing whiskeys directly out of the little bottles. He made no move to stop the flight attendant as he scooped up the bottles before the plane could make it to the runway. In the back row, a grandmotherly type was playing cards with a young girl no older than ten. On the port side of the cabin, Noonan shared his back row with a man who was sound asleep against the window. Noonan couldn't see anything of the four people in front of him save the backs of their heads.

As soon as the plane was aloft, the flight attendant, still smarting from having his schedule adjusted by a tardy passenger, made it back to offer him a drink. Noonan declined, cursing the fact he was on his way to an assignment. He did take a cup of coffee and launched back into his book of Alaska tales. He had just finished the story of the fossilized alligator of Talkeetna as the plane touched down at San Francisco International Airport.

"So much for my Alaska holiday," he muttered as he stuck the book in the inside pocket of his overcoat. "Now, let's see what fate has in store for me."

Chapter 2

Noonan was barely down the Alaska Airlines walkway from the plane in San Francisco, being hustled along in the river of passengers trying to get out of the aircraft, when he was approached by a tall man with gray hair waving a copy of Noonan's book in the boarding area.

"This is getting to be a habit," Noonan mumbled to himself. When his agent had told him he could expect to find people searching him out for an autograph, he had thought she was kidding. She had not been. The book had been out less than a month and there were already people stopping him on street corners and luncheonette counters asking for a signature. It made undercover work impossible.

"Captain Noonan!" The man enthusiastically waving the book had a pen in hand as well. Noonan pulled himself out of the swarm of passengers and stepped into the waiting area.

"I'm certainly glad I caught you here. I couldn't afford to go to Sandersonville, North Carolina, to look for you!"

Noonan smiled and took the man's pen and book. "It's nice to know so many people care."

"Oh, we do. You're a living legend, Captain Noonan. Particularly to us in the law and order business. Will you be in town long?"

The bulk of the passengers were still flooding into the waiting area and bumping into the pair, so they moved a few steps closer to the check-in desk.

"No. Just a few days. Then I'm off on a vacation to Alaska. Seeing in-laws and fishing for king salmon." Noonan emphasized the word king.

Noonan had the man hold his signature leather jacket while he autographed the book. Then he handed the book and pen back to the admirer. "Be sure to buy lots of copies and make me rich and famous."

The man laughed pleasantly. "We can't afford that. There are too many bad guys out there." He waved his autographed book at Noonan. "Thank you, Captain Noonan. It was a pleasure meeting you."

The Matter of the Vanishing Greyhound

Noonan indicated he was going for his luggage, and the man wished Noonan the best and disappeared into the stream of passengers.

It was sweltering in San Francisco, or at least so it seemed to Noonan. Prepared for a cool July in Alaska, he found San Francisco stifling. Having been in the city by the bay many times, he noted with a mixture of delight and disdain it was a beautiful day. San Francisco was one of those doubly blessed cities. When it is wet and cold, as was usually the case, it is a pleasant city with a stable temperature. People dress for the weather and San Franciscans are thus some of the best-dressed people in the United States. Further, because San Francisco is notorious for its fog and rain, when they occur, no one feels as though they have been cheated out of a good day.

Then, on clear warm days, the city becomes one of the most beautiful in America. The little ticky-tacky houses, the term coined by Pete Seegar back when "San Francisco" and "hippies" were synonymous, explode into bright colors turning San Francisco's fabled hills into a checkerboard of Sherwin-Williams paints. Even the roofing material was different shades of red, black and brown.

Today it was hot and stifling. Even the air conditioning in the terminal was not enough to keep the temperature inside from reaching into the 80s. Noonan rejoined the flow of passengers down the terminal corridor toward the luggage carousels, past the restrooms and cul-de-sacs where passengers-to-be were sleeping on suitcases or sprawled across adjacent chairs reading newspapers. He was about to go past one of the bookstores set into the terminal wall when he stopped.

Stepping inside, he wandered about in the boutique before picking up a copy of the *Seattle Times*. Then he walked over to the nonfiction section looking for his book. The little sign over the bookshelf read, "If You Don't See It, Ask."

So he did.

"Do you have any copies of NOONAN'S LAW?"

"No. The title doesn't even ring a bell."

"I see. Thanks." He dropped a dollar bill on the counter for the paper. The clerk said he needed another 50 cents for the paper, so Noonan dug into his pocket for change. Then he rejoined the stampede of passengers to the luggage area. He only stopped once more, this time at the Arrivals/Departure board where he stood for a moment before shaking his head sadly and moving on.

Chapter 2

For someone who had been hustled aboard a San Francisco-bound airplane by the Commissioner himself, Noonan was surprised he had not been met in the terminal lounge. It wasn't so much he expected royal treatment; it was just that he was flying blind. He had not been told why he was going to San Francisco or whom he was supposed to meet. All he knew was he was going to San Francisco and here he was.

As to the crime, all he knew for sure was a bank had been robbed and ten hostages had disappeared. This was certainly strange because hostages were usually used as bargaining chips. But if the perps already had the money and were gone, then the perps did not need the hostages. If this was actually the case, why hold the hostages at all? This could only mean there was something else on the table.

Noonan watched the river of oddly shaped suitcases, bags, boxes, duffels, igloos, and trunks as they disgorged from the basement of the terminal and followed each other one-after-the-next onto the rubber plates of the luggage carousel. When his bags finally made their appearance, he grabbed the handles while the bags were still in motion and shouldered his way out of the luggage area to the street.

Not knowing whom he was going to meet was not a pressing problem. He knew the Chief of the San Francisco Police well so it was just a matter of getting downtown. After that, well, San Francisco, "where little cable cars climb halfway to the stars," was also the city of rude cabbies, smelly shuttle buses and car rental agencies overcharging for everything from clunkers to limos. The only question he had was whether he should be renting a car or waiting to see what developed at Chief Thayer's office. He stepped out onto the sidewalk and began looking into traffic for a familiar face, uniform, or empty cab, whichever came first.

He had no trouble spotting Chief Thayer leaning against the curbside of his squad car with his bubble gum lights flashing. Alongside the curb where the Chief had parked was a bright red strip next to a sign proclaiming NO PARKING.

"Nothing like attracting a bit of attention, eh?" Noonan looked over the crowd of cold stares of the stampede of passengers who had to lug their baggage across the street in the heat into the parking garage. Since Noonan wasn't in cuffs, it was clear to the pedestrians this ride from the curbside was a courtesy.

"Heinz! Sorry, I'm late. It's been absolute heck since this broke. I've been up for over 30 hours. Am I happy you decided to come south! We need you."

"Always glad to help. Rough, eh?"

"Oh, yes." Chief Thayer shook his head sadly. "Not getting any easier either." The Chief grabbed both pieces of luggage and gently placed them in the trunk of his patrol car. "We still don't know where the hostages are. Have you been filled in?"

"Not a word, George. My Commissioner just pulled me off a flight to Alaska and put me on the San Francisco shuttle. I couldn't reach anyone from the plane so I'm flying blind. I'm going to have my staff send me some clothes. All I've got are these vacation duds." Noonan tapped his lapels – or where his lapels should have been.

"Not a problem, Heinz. Why with your reputation you'll probably have this solved and be out of town by midnight anyway. At least that's what I'm hoping."

"George, you have always been an optimist."

Noonan draped his overcoat on top of the two suitcases in the trunk and then latched the back cover. The Chief got into the car and unlocked the passenger side door from the inside. Noonan let the heat vent out of the car before he settled inside.

"So much for a nice cool day," Noonan mused as he strapped his seat belt on while the Chief peered into the oncoming traffic.

"I don't have any time to offer you the niceties of the city, which I apologize for, Heinz. But I'm up to my ears in this one. We're going right to the crime scene."

"Fine with me. I'd hate to come all this way and not have a case to work on."

The Chief looked sideways and laughed. "You haven't changed a bit. We really need you on this one, Heinz. We're not even halfway into this and stumped already."

"Well, no one has told me anything beyond the report you've had a bank robbery in the range of $10 million and ten hostages have been taken."

The Chief shook his head sadly. "That's the good news. The bad news is the take might be as high as $20 million and we've lost the perps and the hostages."

"Exactly what happened?"

"The people who pulled this off were slick. They not only knew what we were going to do, they've been a dozen steps ahead of us all the way. I'm stretched so thin I had to pick you up myself."

"Who else knows I'm in on this? I mean, my coming here was a spur-of-the-moment command decision, right?"

Chapter 2

"Yes it was. It was a routine robbery last night – perps inside with hostages. Nothing unusual." The Chief smiled wryly. "I mean we do have our hostage negotiating team. We finally got a negotiated settlement, a Greyhound to San Francisco International. We followed the bus, at a discrete distance, and suddenly the perps changed their minds. They wanted to go to Sausalito. Across the Golden Gate Bridge. We allowed them to change their destination, of course."

"Of course."

"You and your wry humor, Heinz. Yeah, well, we followed them at a reasonable distance. About ten blocks from the Golden Gate, the bus started spewing smoke. I mean really smoking. We followed the bus onto the bridge. The smoke stops. We stop. The smoke clears. The bus is gone. It entered the bridge. It never left the bridge. Either side. That's when we called you."

"Has anything happened since you called me?"

"We found three bungee cords dangling from the bridge when the sun came up. We're assuming they are associated with the robbery, but we don't know for sure. We've got patrol boats in the water looking for swimmers and we're dragging the channel bottom immediately under the bridge but the current's pretty wicked down there."

"I thought you guys had video cameras set up on the Golden Gate Bridge to stop jumpers."

"We do. But they don't show anything."

"Nothing?"

"Not a thing. The tapes just showed an empty bridge."

"How about the cameras closest to the entrance to the bridge on the San Francisco side. Didn't it show anything?"

"Not a thing. It didn't even show the smoke."

"You checked the equipment?"

"It's being checked again as we speak."

"Did you have a chopper in the sky?"

"Sure did. It followed the bus right onto the bridge. There was also a homing device on the Greyhound. Standard procedure. The homing device indicated the bus went onto the bridge."

"Have you heard anything about the hostages?"

"Not a word."

The two men fell to silence for a long moment. The only sound in the Chief's car was the blast of the air conditioner and the occasional crackle of voices on the police radio. Outside, the high-speed staccato of the wheels on the corrugated pavement drummed monotonously. As the men sat silent, San Francisco Bay ran along the right side of the automobile while on the left, the city began to rise out of Foster City. Cement walls separated the eight lanes of traffic from the houses on both sides of the freeway. Cars of all sizes and horsepower blasted by the Chief who kept a constant 55 miles per hour regardless of who passed.

The freeway changed its heading slightly and sunlight suddenly burned its way across the front windshield. Instantaneously both men adjusted their sun visors. The silence was so oppressive the Chief glanced sideways, almost expecting Noonan to be asleep.

He was not.

The Chief said nothing and the pregnant silence continued.

Finally Noonan broke into the conversation. "A few questions and then I want to recap everything I know."

"Shoot."

"At what time did you know there had been a break-in at the bank?"

The Chief scratched his head for a moment. "Actually, we don't know what time the four perps entered the bank. They were able to circumvent the bank's alarm and were waiting for the bank employees when they arrived on Monday morning. For all we know they could have been in the vault all weekend." He coughed. "They went through the safety deposit boxes methodically so they may very well have been there all weekend. They nabbed the employees one at a time when they came to work, put them in the vault and waited until they had the whole crew. Then one of the perps called us."

"How did the perps get into the bank in the first place? Didn't the bank have a time lock on its vault?"

"Well, there was no sign of a forced entry into the bank or the bank vault so we can only assume it was an inside job. We're checking former employees and vault personnel. As far as we know the bank vault combination is only known by three people. One of them went on vacation last week in the Bahamas. The other two were at the bank on Friday and Monday so we're going over their past, present and future with a fine-tooth comb. But for the moment we're stumped. The guy in the Bahamas is on his way back to San Francisco, by the way, and the other two are hostages. For the moment, we've got nothing to work on. Any one of them could have been the inside man."

"And the time lock?"

"Supposedly the bank has one on the vaults – there are two vaults, one for money and the other for the safety deposit boxes. Somehow the perps went around both of them. Don't ask me how, I don't know. But my people are working on it. There's a good chance the time lock wasn't turned on, once again, probably courtesy of the inside man."

"How about all the other security devices? I'm talking about the motion detectors, odor detectors and all those other newfangled devices. Video cameras? Wasn't someone watching those cameras over the weekend? What about Monday morning when the employees were being picked off one at a time?" Noonan scratched his beard.

"All of the detectors inside the bank were turned off. As far as the video cameras were concerned, yes, there were security people watching the screens all weekend long. Why didn't they see anything? Because the inside man had them watching last weekend's videos which, of course, showed nothing."

"Of course."

"On Monday, while the employees were being rounded up, they were watching last Thursday's video. When the perps made their call, the video cameras went dead."

"What about last Friday's videotape? I'll bet that's gone."

"Right. That's what we asked for too. We figured it would show the perps being let into the bank by the inside man."

"That's kind of the way I would have figured it." Captain Noonan stretched and turned toward the window and watched the cement wall running along the freeway. They were driving in the far right lane now and Noonan couldn't see over the retaining wall. The view was an ongoing sheet of gray-brown concrete broken only by the equally spaced joints where the blocks had been slid together. "So the perps were in place at 10 a.m. How many were there?"

"Four. That's how many came out with the hostages. We talked with one who was a male. We don't know about the others. When they came out of the bank they were moving with the hostages so we really don't have a clue. But we guess at least one was female. But that's a guess based on the way the individual walked. Other than that we don't know."

"What was the name of the male on the phone?"

"He didn't give one. He just referred to himself as the man in the bank."

"Smart."

"Worse than that, he was just wasting time. He knew he wasn't going anywhere until at least midnight so he spent his time pretending to be nervous, uncertain, paranoid, all of the signs of a perp breaking down. Looking back on it, the guy was a real pro. He knew exactly what we would do and when. Almost as though he had read one of our manuals."

"Maybe he had. What time did the perps actually leave the bank?"

"About midnight. Then they…"

Noonan held up his hand. "No. Not so fast. I've got to take this slowly. Now, back to inside of the bank. I gather you really don't know anything about the events in the bank because the hostages are missing."

"Right." There was a pause for a moment. "That is an embarrassment."

"I can understand that. But, personally, look at it this way. Those perps have been planning this robbery for months, maybe years. They waited for the right set of circumstances and the right instant of time. They figured you would react by the book, and you did. You fell into their trap because you were doing your job."

"That still doesn't get me much."

"Not right now. But what is keeping those perps one step ahead of you is they know what they are doing and you don't. We're only 30 hours into this and we've got a long way to go before it's over."

This softball didn't seem to impress the Chief at all. He slammed his hands on the steering wheel and cursed. He was silent for a moment and started to say something. Noonan stopped him.

"No need to say it. It's easy to say we should of or we could have but these perps were well ahead of you at the starting gate. Now it's a catchup game. See, the average cop, whether he's a Chief of police or a probationary patrolman can make mistakes, do stupid things. We're not all bright all the time. But a cop is only stupid until the end of his shift. Then he's got time to think, analyze what went wrong, think about the possibilities and then talk with other cops. It's the think time and talking that makes the difference because 90 percent of being a good cop is from the shoulders up. Your problem is that you haven't come to the end of your shift yet. You've put in 30 hard hours without a break. You're too tired to think straight. When we get to the crime scene, you get some sleep. You'll be amazed at what eight hours of shut eye can do for the thinking process."

"But I don't.".. .

"I just need you to finish with the bank. We don't know what went on inside because none of the hostages came out. But if they were in there all day the hostages must have eaten something, gone to the bathroom, stretched their legs."

"The man in the bank told us the hostages were being fed and allowed to go to the bathroom – he called it the loo but he didn't have an accent so I suspect he was using the English word for bathroom to throw us onto a false scent. I'm sure they were all allowed to go to the bathroom when they needed to because we didn't find any evidence to the contrary."

"Food?"

"Whether or not anything was eaten we don't know yet. We assume everyone inside did eat something. When the perps left they took bags with them and in one, or several, of those bags was their garbage. They didn't leave any trash behind. Probably afraid of leaving fingerprints."

"Has the lab finished going over the vaults?"

"Yeah. They found quite a few fingerprints but we're betting those are from the employees. But they found more hair and fiber evidence than we'll ever be able to track."

"What do you mean by that?"

"Well, clearly the perps expected us to send in our hair and fiber people. So they flooded whatever incidental hair and fiber they might have left with false trails. They must have been collecting hair from barbershops and fiber from carpets for weeks. I mean, the minute we got inside it was obvious. By sheer volume they have defeated the hair and fiber people. There's no way we could analyze every strand of hair we found on the floor and make any meaningful comparison."

"How did the perps get into the safety deposit boxes?"

"The old fashion way, hammer and chisel. It took quite a bit of time but they had all the time they needed. Every box was hit and every box was looted carefully. It wasn't like they opened a box and then spilled the contents to find the goodies. They were methodical – and precise – and took everything of value. Jewelry, knick-knacks, coins. Everything. We didn't find anything on the floor of the safety deposit vault but empty boxes, steel chips and lots and lots of paper which has no value, like wills, deeds, stock certificates, stuff like that."

"The money vault?"

"They had two hostages who had the key and the combination so there wasn't any need to be clever about that."

"You said the initial estimate was about $10 million was taken. Why so high? I know this is San Francisco but ten million in cash is still a good chunk of change."

"You're right. We wondered about the amount too. According to Butterfield-Fargo First, the money, cash in this case, was kept on hand at the request of a single client, English Petroleum."

"English Petroleum? Matches with the word loo at the very least."

The Chief gave a sick smile. "We made that connection too and logged it. We checked with English Petroleum and they confirmed they had made the request for the cash. But they wouldn't tell us why."

"Any ideas why they would keep so much money in cash and on hand?"

"The only one we could come up with was cash for bribes in foreign countries. English Petroleum can't legally buy off any of the local constabulary in some Third World countries." The Chief shook his head sadly. "But that's just a guess."

"So they jiggled their books and a million here and there drops out of the system. Cash makes no enemies, eh?"

The Chief looked sideways for an instant. "Not yet but I'll bet the IRS is going to have a field day with English Petroleum."

Noonan smiled sardonically. "It couldn't happen to nicer people. But that's still a big chunk of change to have in a vault of a Cracker Jack bank. How was English Petroleum going to move it?"

The Chief was about to respond but for the moment he was too busy with driving. They left the freeway and began to wind their way through streets of San Francisco. It was still stifling in the car. Noonan opened the window possibly under the illusion it was cooler outside. He was in error and he rolled the glass back up as soon as he realized it wasn't any cooler outside. The Chief smiled and shook his head humorously.

As soon as the Chief felt comfortable with the traffic he responded to the query Noonan had given him on the freeway. "They said they needed to move it one million at a time. They had already made arrangements with an armored car security van. The first shipment was to be yesterday, the day of the robbery."

"Was this the first time they had put so much money in this bank?"

"In this particular bank, yes. But they've deposited as much cash in other banks around San Francisco in the past."

"That's still a load even a million at a time. What were the denominations?"

"Hundreds. All sequentially numbered. That's the only good news. At least we can trace the bills."

"Maybe." Noonan was clearly not impressed. "What size of a pile would $10 million in one hundred dollar bills make?"

Chief Thayer thought for a moment. "Well, a bundle of one hundred dollar bills is about the size of a brick and is worth $10,000. One million in 100 bills is 100 bricks and $10 million is 1,000 bricks."

"All together it'd be pretty heavy." Noonan whistled softly. "Then there are all the goodies from the safety deposit boxes. I guess they needed the hostages to carry the loot."

"And the garbage," the Chief said. "That's a load for 14 people."

"Maybe too much of a load." Noonan patted his shirt pocket and then started to dig in his pants pocket clearly looking for a pen.

The Chief patted his shirt pockets and, when he found no pen, popped open the glove compartment. "See if you find one in there."

While the Chief may have been slow on the freeway, he was in his element in the city. He handled the auto like a cowboy on a stallion chasing a stampede of thundering steer down into arroyos and through draws only to crest another arroyo. The car bounced in potholes, slid on cobblestones, jitterbugged through construction zones and then whined as it strove to climb the mighty hills of San Francisco. Bouncing across tram tracks and zipping through intersections, he drove into the Mission District and then into the Sunset District south of Golden Gate Park.

While the Chief was dodging fast dogs and slow pedestrians, Noonan plowed through the trash in the glove box, looking for a pen or pencil in the sea of plastic knives, soy sauce packages, paper salt-and-pepper packages, napkins and a flashlight. After he found the pencil he double-folded a napkin and began his calculations. "Let's see, each brick weighs about 1.2 pounds and there are 1,000 bricks. That's 1,200 pounds divided by 14 people makes about 85 pounds per person."

The Chief shook his head sadly. "You're right. I do need to sleep. We watched 14 people leave the bank, all with backpacks. But they couldn't have been carrying 85 pounds per person. Some of the hostages were women. At the max we're talking about an average of 30 pounds per person. Thirty times fourteen is three times 140 or 500 pounds."

Noonan fiddled with the paper. "OK, Five hundred pounds. Now, let's talk about food. They had to come in with enough food for four people for three days plus ten people for one day. Figuring three meals a day for the four perps is 12 meals a day times three days is 36 meals. Add 20 more meals for the 10 hostages. That's 56 meals and say each meal yields a pound and a half of garbage. All together there's about a hundred pounds. Which leaves another 400 to 450 pounds for the safety deposit box goodies. I'm assuming no one came out with a pushcart."

"No one did. So the $10 million is still in the bank somewhere."

"Maybe not." Noonan scratched his beard with the pencil butt. "Or probably not. There's our inside man again. That's probably why the Friday night tape is gone. The bank closes, our inside man and the four perps roll out the $10 million in cash in a cart. They could have done it in an hour."

The Chief shook his head as he gripped the wheel in anger. "Damn! We've been looking at this too hard. We're missing the obvious."

"That's why you call in the outsiders, Chief. I'll bet if you ever do find the Friday tape it's going to show the four perps dressed as armored car employees. They might have even rented an armored car for their cover. The security people at the bank aren't going to report anything because there is nothing unusual to report. They've been told there's going to be some money taken out of the bank and there was."

"But there had to be some paperwork," Chief Thayer said. "You can't just take out $10 million in cash and not leave some kind of a trail."

"True. True." Noonan diddled on the paper. "But it's a pretty good bet the perps took paperwork out the door with the garbage."

The Chief snapped his fingers. "But if that were the case, why were the perps in the bank over the weekend? I don't see a good reason."

"Unless they wanted what was in the safety deposit boxes," Noonan added. "They had the time so why not get as much as they could? They got greedy. They could have just left the paperwork where it was."

Chief Thayer thought about it. "They could have been gone an hour before the bank opened on Monday. If they were clever enough to have maneuvered around the time locks, the front door would have been a Cracker Jack box. They could have moved all of the trash and the safety deposit box contents out in two trips, say 65 or 70 pounds per person."

"If they had left their trash in the bank it would have been even less. There's something we're missing here, George. There is some reason they needed us to spin our wheels for a while."

"We've been spinning our wheels since the hostages were taken and the camera lenses sprayed."

"You didn't tell me that. The cameras were sprayed with paint?"

"Right. We don't have any video of what went on in the bank all day."

The Chief was about to continue when he gave a great yawn and suddenly pulled up at a curb. "We're here and I'm going to take your advice and get some sleep. I'm getting batty."

Noonan turned sideways toward the Chief. Noonan loosened his seat belt and stopped the Chief from loosening his. "Sleep, Chief. That's a great idea. Don't come back until you're rested," Noonan put his hand on the Chief's elbow. "Really rested. We need you at the top of your game."

Noonan turned and reached toward the door handle on the passenger side of the patrol car. Before his hand could come in contact with the handle, the door was pulled open from the outside. A blast of wet heat engulfed him. "So much for air conditioning," Noonan muttered. Noonan turned and looked through the opening door. There, in the expanding crack between the patrol car frame and the door was a man who was the spitting image of Baby Huey.

Baby Huey was extending a hand toward Noonan, "Captain Noonan. I'd recognize you anywhere. I'm Douglas Hopkins of Capital Assurance and Fidelity, Inc. We're the people who have to pay if you don't find the money."

"You've got a lot of faith in a man you've never met," Noonan said.

Douglas Hopkins was a pudgy six feet tall, about 30 years old, had the doughy face of a man who looked as though he had never missed a meal or a good night's sleep and had yet to meet a gymnasium he would enter. In spite of the fact Noonan was sweating like a Sumo wrestler – and he, Noonan, was from North Carolina and used to humidity – Hopkins appeared cool. At least he was not sweating even though he was wearing a suit. Part of the reason could have been his short cropped, curly hair. His clothes were perfectly preserved as if he had just stepped out of a dry cleaners, and he had manicured nails. His shoes were leather, expensive and shined. This was odd, Noonan thought, because there are only six days a year when San Franciscans can wear shoes that are leather and shined.

Hopkins helped Noonan out of the patrol car. Noonan turned back to the Chief and caught him in a yawn. "Get some sleep," Noonan said and the Chief nodded.

Noonan was still shaking Hopkins' hand as he loosened his collar with his free hand. Stepping up onto the curb, the "Bearded Holmes" shrugged his shoulders to pull his shirt away from his back where it had become plastered. As he was standing on the curb becoming acclimated to the heat, the Chief leaned across the front seat of the car.

"I've got you booked at the St. Francis, Heinz. I'll have your bags taken up to your room. I'll catch up with you when I can. Hopkins will introduce you around."

"Fine," responded Noonan as he stepped back off the curb and put his hands on the roof of the car. The heat made him withdraw his hands quickly. Leaning into the car he extended his right hand to the Chief. "It's always nice to be San Francisco, George, even when it's hot."

The Chief nodded 'good-bye' as Noonan slammed the passenger side door and hit the roof of the patrol car. The Chief waved inside the car as he careened down the street, made a sharp right and disappeared.

For a moment the street was silent.

Noonan stepped up onto the sidewalk and took a slow look around the intersection. Hopkins stood silently beside him, respectful as if here were at a funeral and the family of the deceased had just arrived.

Dominating one corner was Butterfield-Fargo First. The structure itself was short and squat, a dirty gray building dominating the approaches of both streets, Kalloch and De Young. There were windows on the facing walls, one for each street, and the entry way was in a setback at the apex of the streets. The second floor had no windows; it was just a cement box set on top of the bank.

From where he stood on the corner, Noonan could see the line of boutiques disappearing down both side streets. They were all set into what appeared to be one, long, cement wall running from street corner to street corner. From where he stood it was clear the entire block was a single cement building. Brightly colored, the small stores were set shoulder-to-shoulder-to-shoulder with their display windows so close to each other it reminded him of a beach community, like Laguna or Seaside, where the businesses were small because they had to make maximum profit with minimum floor space. Most of the boutiques had settled for putting their names flush to the cement wall but there were a few signs erected on the roof.

Catty-corner from the bank and running halfway down Kalloch Avenue was an anonymous gray, three-story structure, the generic office building which rented offices by the week or month. Windows, most of them open, marked the walls like the tracks of a junkie. The building was stained all along the bottom, from the entryway all to the way to the end of the emergency exits on both sides, almost as if someone had sloshed paint gently into the vortex where building and sidewalk joined. There was some

Chapter 2

innocent graffiti near one of the emergency exits, "John 3:3" and "666." On both facing streets boutiques dominated the balance of the block, all generic in appearance.

What was left of a command post was clearly visible on the roof of the three-story building opposite the bank. On both sides of the billboard, which dominated the street – reminding San Franciscans that "Friends Don't Let Friends Drive Drunk" with an inane illustration that did not deliver the message – were two barricades. Three SWAT members, their rifles casually slung over their shoulders, lounged on the rooftop. One was smoking.

On street level, yellow police tape still marked off the Butterfield-Fargo First property. Noonan walked the length of the building in silence, Hopkins following at his heels like a puppy dog. When Noonan returned to the bank's entrance, two of the dozen San Francisco policemen stepped forward to stop him when he tried to duck under the tape but Hopkins waved them back. One of the men handed Noonan a pair of latex gloves, which he slid on as he walked into the bank unhindered.

The interior of Butterfield-Fargo looked like the inside of a Cracker Jack box and was built that way. There were two vault doors at the deep end with a single counter of tellers' cages which ran the length of the room. With the electricity turned off, a remnant of the siege, the only light in the building oozed in through the grit on the double windows on each side of the entryway. The only things lacking for an authentic 1930s movie set were cobwebs in the room corners and machine-gun bullet holes in a string along the back wall. A threadbare rug, brown of color or age, covered the floor like a shallow swamp. The branch manager's desk wallowed at the back of the room between the vault doors like a toad up to its elbows in stagnant water. At the right rear was a single door, wide enough to admit a forklift. To Noonan's right was a pair of restrooms, which looked as though they had been salvaged from a Greyhound bus station.

Noonan knelt for a moment and used a pencil to pick through what appeared to be a clump of dust. It was actually matted hair. Looking around he saw there was hair everywhere, mixed with odd-colored fibers. He rose and picked his way along the counter to the vaults. After he had inspected both vaults, he returned to the main room. It was at this point Hopkins made his second introduction of the day. He extended his Latex glove covered hand as he stepped forward.

"Douglas Hopkins, Chief. I'm with..."

29

Noonan took his hand again and gave it a sturdy shake. "Capital Assurance and Fidelity. Yes, I know. Just because I seem preoccupied don't be distracted."

"Not at all, sir."

"Please. Call me Captain Noonan, or Noonan, or Heinz but don't call me sir. Even my father won't let me call him sir."

"Sounds fair to me," Hopkins said as he swept the room with his free hand. "This doesn't look like much of a bank, does it?"

"Exactly what I was thinking, Douglas."

"Call me Doug." "OK.

"Oh, this is a bank all right. At least in name and insurance."

Noonan pointed to the counter running along the wall. "It looks as though Butterfield-Fargo First found an abandoned bank and refurbished it. This is not exactly the section of town I would have expected to find a Butterfield-Fargo bank. These guys are known for class, style, culture and finesse. This neighborhood has all the sophistication of Velveeta nachos."

Hopkins reached into his jacket pocket and pulled out a business card he handed to Noonan. "You're right about one thing. This bank was picked up on a foreclosure and refurbished by Butterfield-Fargo. About two years ago. We checked the vaults and the security system before they made the purchase. We made some recommendations. The bank followed them to the letter and we gave the bank a clean bill of health."

Noonan didn't say anything. He glanced at Hopkins card and stuck it in his pants pocket. Then he continued his survey of the room, starting with the ceiling tiles and working his way down the walls to the floor. Hopkins gave a look indicating he understood Noonan was making the inventory but continued to speak.

"Yes, it's sold. Yes, the vaults are used. But the security system was upgraded."

Noonan walked over to the security camera and looked up at a spray-painted lens.

Hopkins correctly guessed at what he was thinking. "That's right. They hit all the lenses with spray paint. Poof. One quick blast per camera, *psfaat*, and there went our inside eye."

Noonan scuffed his way over to the counter, Hopkins following him. Finally Noonan addressed Hopkins. "Chief Thayer took me as far as the bank. I take it the one perp who was on the phone diddled all day long, stretching out the negotiations."

"Right. We couldn't figure out what he was doing until the sun went down and he still didn't have any demands."

"How did you get the tip the bank was being taken down?"

"The security people reported the video lenses had been sprayed," Hopkins pointed at the cameras. "It was at about 10 a.m. When the bank didn't open, people called. Then the police got a call from one of the perps. Then the craziness started."

"The perps called the cops? That's a bit odd." Noonan looked at Hopkins strangely.

"If we're starting a list of odd things about this case, the perp calling the police is down about Number 27." Hopkins gave a nervous laugh.

Noonan cracked a smile and pointed at the video cameras. "Where are the actual video machines, the screens themselves?"

"A private security company. They monitor everything, keep the tapes."

Noonan cut him off. "But the Friday tape is missing. How close do they monitor the tapes? Do they make back-ups?"

"Losing the Friday tape was a bummer. It was there on Saturday because it was logged in. When it disappeared we don't know. Whoever took the tape understood the security system. I don't know what the Chief told you but we did find a tape in the Friday slot. But it was the tape from two Fridays ago. The security company keeps all tapes for a week, just in case something like this happens. Then they use the oldest tape to make the newest one. The Friday tape we saw came from two Fridays ago. We speculate someone switched the old Friday tape in question with a blank tape. No one was going to be examining an old tape before it's re-used so a blank one was as good as a used one. No one would know the difference. Then he replaced last Friday's tape with the previous Friday's."

"You know it was a man?"

"She. It could have been a she."

"How many bank people could have gotten into the office where the security tapes are located?"

"Three. Two of the possibilities are hostages and the third is, was, in the Bahamas. All three are male so I guess we don't have to be P.C. about the inside man. Every one of them had motive, opportunity and means, MOM, the cornerstone of prosecution."

"Was the Friday tape you have dusted?"

"We had all the tapes dusted. The Friday tape was clean. The other tapes had the fingerprints of the security guard personnel."

Noonan tapped his pencil rhythmically on the end of his nose.

Hopkins broke the silence. "The perps had everything going for them as long as they keep moving. Every time they can do anything to confuse us, even for 15 minutes, that's time they can use to their advantage. We ran through the tape twice before we realized we were watching the wrong Friday."

Hopkins continued, "The bottom line for these guys is they need time to pull this off. That's why they still have the hostages. We don't know where they are or what they are going to do. Every second we spend spinning our wheels is a second to their advantage."

Noonan turned and faced Hopkins. "These do not appear to be your normal perps. Why do you think they took hostages? They've got the money and the loot from the bank vault. They've got what they wanted; why take hostages?"

Hopkins shook his head. "Not a clue. Except to stall us. As long as we are looking for the hostages we are not looking for them."

"True. True." Noonan slipped the pencil into his pocket and peered down the counter and brushed it. He looked at the heel of his hand and then showed it to Hopkins. "We also have a problem on our end. Laziness. What do you see here?"

Hopkins looked at the Noonan's hand and shrugged his shoulders. "I don't know what you're getting at. I don't see anything."

"Precisely. What you should see is white powder, the dusting for fingerprints. That's pretty sloppy police work. What we have here is a major crime, loss of about $10 million in cash and valuables, ten lives at risk and the lab people are getting lazy."

"They probably felt . . ."

"Hopkins! Solving a crime is only half of the job. The second is getting a conviction. Now I can understand your point of view. You're in the insurance business. If the $10 million in cash and all the goodies from the safety deposit boxes come back, you're pleased as punch. But I," Noonan tapped his chest, "and the Chief have to worry about getting a conviction. We've got some pretty careful customers here. Extra hair on the floor, all the trash taken out, tapes missing, escape vehicle vanishing. What this tells me is when we catch these guys we're going to have a heck of a fight in court. Slipshod work like this," he shook his open hand which should have been coated with the white powder it had picked up when he swept the counter, "won't get us a conviction."

Hopkins was silent for a moment. "It's not true I'm not worried about..."

"Spare me, Hopkins. Let's get to the root of the problem now. I've seen what I want to see, now let's talk about the getaway."

Hopkins started to speak and Noonan silenced him with a wave. "Just because I seem to be working a little slow here doesn't mean I don't know what kind of time pressure we're under. I have to approach the problem methodically. But I'm well aware of the time element. I don't know this city but I do know perps. My job is to figure out what happened and hope there's a clue to where the hostages are. While I'd like to be polite and observe all the social graces, I don't have the time. What happened here?"

If Hopkins was taken aback, he didn't show it. So he answered Noonan's question. "Well, we surrounded the bank with the usual. SWAT and squad cars, men at the front and back, sound detectors, gas masks, the whole nine yards. We even had Spanish and Chinese speaking detectives just in case. Here in San Francisco you never know who you're going to be speaking to when you are called into a hot zone."

"Hot zone?"

"That's what we call it here. It's what the insurance companies call it. I don't know what the police call it."

"Good enough. How about the press?"

"Those guys were all over us like white on rice. We're talking about being on the scene at 10:25 in the a.m., Hey they were off-loading cameras as the cops were tumbling out of their vans."

"How did they get the word?"

"They said they got an anonymous call. They were here all day, until they sent their footage in for the 11:00 news. Then they went home, left a cub reporter or two. That's when the perps made their move."

"Was there any shooting at any time?"

"No, thank God, because those yo-yos were doing newscasts exposed with the bank at their back to the plate glass windows of the bank. I mean, come on! Everyone in San Francisco with the IQ of a turnip knew which bank was going down. Everyone knew so everyone and his brother showed up. We had a packed sidewalk! One shot from inside the bank and the slug would have hit four, five people. Then we had the usual carloads of looky-loos driving around the police lines, snapping selfies and shooting home video footage. You just can't keep those people away. The police lines don't mean anything anymore."

"Then?"

33

"The perps got here before ten in the morning and stayed until about midnight. There isn't much to report about those hours. We never saw them and we only talked to one man. At first the perp hemmed and hawed about how he was holding hostages. Then he apologized. Then he wouldn't speak to us for a few hours. He wouldn't answer the phone when we called in so we had to wait until he called us."

"Was it always the same perp?"

"Same guy."

"This went on all day?"

"Right. Until about midnight."

"Exactly what happened when the perps finally cut a deal?"

"After hours of negotiations we finally cut a deal with them. The one guy we were talking to said he wanted a Greyhound bus out in front of the bank. He said he was going to take the hostages with him and he didn't want to see any cops on any rooftops and he didn't want to see any cops following him."

"The Chief agreed to that?"

"Sure. Why not? SWAT just pulled back from the roof," Hopkins said. He pointed up through the ceiling of the bank as if it were not there to the command post Noonan had seen on the three-story building across the street from the bank. "There was no reason to be seen if the perps were on the move so SWAT pulled back. Then it was up to the motorized units. The bus left and everybody kind of hung back about a block and a half. It's not hard to follow a Greyhound bus in San Francisco!"

"The perps never complained?"

"Oh, they complained right away. They were on a cellular phone. Called right to the Chief on his iPhone. Surprised him right out of his socks. One minute he's ordering the motorized units to move out and the next he's taking guff from the perp on a cellular phone – private, direct number no less. These guys were prepared."

"Clearly. Did the perps say where they were going?"

"They wanted free access to San Francisco International and then they changed their minds. They drove around town for about half an hour like they were lost and then said they wanted to go to Sausalito."

"Sausalito?"

"Yeah, isn't that a hoot?"

"There isn't much of anything in Sausalito, is there?" Noonan looked surprised.

"Nice town, but it doesn't have an airport worth talking about if that's what you mean. There are a lot of boats but it's a town that can be bottled up. But that's where they said they wanted to go. Chief said fine. He figured he could cut them off on the Golden Gate Bridge. He closed off the north entrance, waited for them to get on the bridge and then closed off the south side. Poof, they're bottled up on the bridge. Better to have them there than at the International Airport."

"What went wrong?"

"Good question. The Greyhound got here at the bank about 12:30 and the perps got on board. The Chief gets a call to back off with his men and he does. Besides, he's got a chopper in the air, and a directional bug on the Greyhound. He's got a SWAT team at the International Airport because that's where the perps said they wanted to go. What's he got to worry about? Where are the perps going to go? When they get to the airport they're going to be bottled up."

"So off the bus went, the cops hanging way back and the chopper following the bus?" Noonan asked.

"Right. The bus headed south and suddenly the perps changed their minds. They cut back across town and began zigzagging through the city. They snapped their headlights off and ran in the dark, up and down hills with the perp yelling he could still see the cops behind him and the bear in the air."

"Did the perp use the term bear in the air?"

"No. I think he used the word chopper or helicopter. Bear in the air is my term."

"So far so good. Now for Houdini."

"Right. Suddenly the perps say they don't trust the arrangements and were going to Sausalito. Chief says fine and orders the Golden Gate closed on the north side. He figures he's going to bottle them up on the bridge. About ten blocks back from the south entrance to the Golden Gate Bridge, the bus starts smoking. Then it really started smoking. The perp on the cellular is now hysterical, yelling the Chief double-crossed him, gave him a two-bit bus which was going to break down, screaming about doing horrible things to the hostages, so the Chief says he won't have his patrol cars enter the bridge from the south."

"Let me guess. The bus, still smoking, blasted onto the bridge. The chopper was still following it and the homing device indicated the bus was on the bridge. Why couldn't the helicopter see the bus? The bridge is all lighted up."

"There was very heavy fog that night. You know how San Francisco can get. When the fog is that thick the lights on the bridge don't even work that well for cars. It was pea soup. Those guys really knew what they were doing. Chose the right night to disappear on the Golden Gate Bridge."

"Right, right, right. So when the cops fought their way through the heavy fog there was no bus on the bridge, the perp dropped off the line and that's the end of the story."

"The bus had just vanished."

"Right. Poof. Gone."

"I'll bet there's no sign of a directional bug or a smoke machine."

"You're batting 1,000 today, Captain."

"Yeah, for what good it does. First things first, I want to go to the last contact spot, where the bus started smoking."

"Not a problem."

"Can you pick your way through the city streets to the spot the way the bus went?"

"Sorry. No can do. The bus was running up one-way streets the wrong way and even went through a tram tunnel. I couldn't risk it."

"But people were following him the whole way." Noonan was intent on this answer.

"The whole way?"

"The chopper had the bus in view the whole way, right, except when it went through those tram tunnels?"

"As far as I know." Hopkins scratched his head and thought for a moment. "Well, sort of, the patrol cars lost track of the bus every now and again when they were ordered to fall back but they were steered back on course by the chopper."

Noonan grunted, brushed his hand against his pants and moved for the front door of the bank with amazing agility for a 60-something-year-old man.

Chapter 3

San Francisco, the tourist destination, was quite a bit different than the San Francisco Captain Noonan was seeing through the front window of the Mercedes 210. He made the comment to Hopkins, who was at the wheel.

"Things always look different through the windshield of a 210," Hopkins said as he honked and cursed at the Sacramento drivers who were making the streets of San Francisco unsafe for the North Beach Yuppies.

Hopkins skirted the south side of Golden Gate Park and whipped through the late afternoon traffic with his tape deck blaring, "Jeremiah was a Bull Frog." Noonan nodded absently to the incessant commentary by Hopkins and watched the pattern of neighborhoods change. They went through Golden Gate Park and then joined the ballet of trucks, buses, motorcycles and autos as they swept north along the Park Presidio Bypass.

"Do you want to drive across the bridge?" Hopkins yelled over the tape. "Once we're on the bridge, we're on it all the way to Sausalito."

Noonan shook his head. "Can we park on the San Francisco side and just walk to the bridge entrance?"

"Yeah! You can walk all the way across if you want to. It's a bit chilly though."

"I only want to walk as far as the three bungees. The ones the Chief says the perps might have used."

"Not a problem." Hopkins looked over his right shoulder and let a bus blast by. Then he headed for the exit on Lincoln Boulevard. The moment they left the parkway, the traffic noise vaporized until it was quiet enough they did not have to yell to be heard in the Mercedes. As soon as he found a parking space, Hopkins pulled over to the curb. When the men stepped out onto the sidewalk, Hopkins chirped the anti-theft device on his car.

"I'll never get used to those things," Noonan said, jumping a bit as he looked over his shoulder. "We don't need them in Sandersonville."

"Welcome to living in a real city, Captain," Hopkins stuck his cellular phone into the inside pocket of his suit. "Got to get used to the big time."

The two men stepped over a shin-high hedge and walked across a vacant lot labeled a park that was pocked with muddy holes drying in the hot sun and stands of foxtails. Glass from broken bottles crunched under their shoes. Noonan pointed out some scattered syringes on the ground, but Hopkins just shrugged. "It's the neighborhood," he said offhandedly. Then he pointed to the rows of deteriorating houses. "Welfare queens. The city's full of them."

"Don't worry," replied Noonan snidely. "I doubt they're insured."

Once across the vacant lot, the men walked a block and a half, and then the sidewalk swept around a dense hedge and suddenly they were on the walkway to the southern entrance of the Golden Gate Bridge. If nothing else, the transition between city and bridge was spectacular. Within a matter of a few yards they had gone from grime and tenements to one of the most beautiful landmarks in America. The bridge, its full majesty beaming in the glory of a sunny day, rose like the rampart of a castle, the drawbridge down, welcoming all who cared to enter the fabled city by the bay. In most places it was a golden yellow but there were splotches of rust here and there on the spans and risers.

As soon as he started across the bridge, Noonan shivered and wished he had brought his jacket. Even though the sun was shining it was surprisingly chilly on the bridge; the up-welling air currents from off the waters of the Golden Gate Bridge tossed his hair as he stood with his back to the bay, the whine of trucks and cars once again making conversation almost impossible.

The walk was much longer than Noonan had anticipated. Hopkins just smiled when Noonan pointed out it felt like they were halfway across the bridge. "Not even," Hopkins yelled above the din of the cars. Finally, 30 yards beyond the first massive girder on the San Francisco end, they came upon a small area marked off with crime scene tape. Hopkins stepped over the tape and pointed to three marks on the bridge railing.

"Here's where the bungees were found," Hopkins shouted above the traffic's roar. "The bungees themselves are back at the lab. The cords themselves were attached under the bridge. The only way we actually spotted them was when the sun came up and we searched the bridge with binoculars from the bayside for a clue. Even then it took us a few hours to spot them. There were weights on the bottoms to keep them straight and taut."

"So no one was watching the perps after they got on the bridge? What about these video cameras? We've passed a handful of them. Didn't they show anything?"

"Not a thing. We're assuming somehow the perps tapped into the cable wires. No one knew they were going to be on the bridge until the last minute so no one was prepared for them to be tampering with the equipment."

Noonan looked back toward the San Francisco side of the bridge and then his eyes trailed over to the Sausalito end. "Too far to have used any kind of night scopes even if you had known."

"That's right," Hopkins said. "Everything happened out here all of a sudden. In fact, we really don't know anything about what happened here at all." Hopkins yelled for a moment to have his voice heard above the roar of a semi loaded with live chickens lurching past them, the stench of manure swirling with white feathers being swept off the animals. "All we know for sure was the police helicopter followed a smoking vehicle onto the bridge. It couldn't get too close because the guy on the bus was yelling about being followed and like I said before, it was pea soup. I'm surprised the chopper could even see the smoke, frankly. The smoking stopped somewhere around here," Hopkins indicated the cords. "We're assuming so. Seemed logical. The bungee cords were here."

Noonan didn't say anything for a moment. "Then the reason you're searching boats along the waterfront is in the hopes they did take a boat?"

"They had to. The water down there is pretty cold and very rough. If they were in the water long, well, they wouldn't be spending any money ever again. We had to wait until the sun came up to start looking. But even if someone had gone down those cords, we still don't know what happened to whatever went onto the bridge. We now know it wasn't the Greyhound. But it was something traveling at 45 miles an hour and it did have a homing device on it and some kind of a smoke machine smoking to beat the band. What do you think happened to the vehicle?"

"Now that is a very good question. Have you started a search of the water down there?" Noonan pointed over the rail at the water 200 feet below.

Hopkins nodded. "Yes, but we won't find anything. It's a couple of hundred feet deep right here and the current along the bottom is vicious. Anything that went down has probably been rolled out to sea – if it's still in one piece. We're looking but we don't expect to have much luck."

"Let's cross."

"What?!" yelled Hopkins incredulously. "Why?"

"I want a different perspective for our walk back."

"It's your funeral." Hopkins shook his head sadly. While Noonan surveyed the bridge, Hopkins pulled his cellular phone from his suit coat and punched in a number. "I don't want anyone thinking we're jumpers," he yelled to Noonan. "And I don't want a squad car checking up on us when the cameras show us sprinting across the bridge."

"Do your job," Noonan muttered as he looked over the edge of the bridge and straight down to the water.

When Hopkins finished the call the two men scaled the newly-constructed ten-foot retaining fence and perched on top like a pair of monkeys in a zoo. The road was almost bumper-to-bumper with cars headed out of San Francisco but on the incoming lanes, the vehicles were scattered. If they could make it across the first three lanes of traffic they wouldn't have any trouble making it to the other side.

The cars were whizzing by at 45 and 50 miles an hour, which did not sit well with Hopkins. He was about to call the scamper off when there was suddenly a momentary lull in the traffic. In an instant Noonan was off the fence and dashing across the traffic lanes of the bridge. Hopkins was caught by surprise and couldn't move as fast as Noonan. While Noonan made it all the way across the six lanes with no difficulty, Hopkins was not so lucky. A split-second behind Noonan, his opening in the traffic was significantly tighter. When he hit the first lane and the serpentine of cars had to slow, their drivers honking horns in anger as Hopkins did a jackrabbit across the three lanes of outgoing traffic. Once across the centerline, Hopkins could walk leisurely to the retaining fence on the other side of the bridge. He put his hands on the cyclone fence to catch his breath. Noonan, already on the far side of the fence, shook his head sadly.

"You're out of shape, Hopkins. Gotta work out every day, cut down on fatty foods, quite smoking, watch salt and sugar and stay away from the hard liquor."

"Thanks, Doc," Hopkins said as he bit the air for breath. "Just what I need is a health lecture." Then he slowly clawed his way up and over the cyclone fence. "You'd figure I was in shape from scuba diving. Apparently that's not the case."

"Where do you skin dive around here? I thought you said the currents were pretty treacherous."

"Here they are. But not up north. Bodega Bay. I've even got a boat up there, the *Cagliostro*."

"The 18th Century alchemist, eh? Very good. I didn't think you insurance guys had a classical education."

"I don't. I got a degree in real estate. But you're the first person I've ever met who knew who Cagliostro was. Where'd you learn that?"

"I have a degree in European history. You never know what tidbits you pick up in life. Bodega Bay's quite a bit north, isn't it? Why not San Francisco Bay or someplace south, like Monterey?"

"It's got abs, that's abalone, and some of the best halibut fishing on the coast. I like to take my tanks and go after but. That's halibut to you people from Sandersonville."

"Oh, we have halibut in Sandersonville. Very big ones. Bigger than those around here. Almost as big as the ones in Alaska. We just fish for them out of a boat."

"Not the same as fishing with a speargun." Hopkins watched as Noonan looked over the rail at the water below.

The trip back to the car was a bit slower. Noonan led the way, stopping occasionally as he peered down over the rail or ran his fingers along the railing and fence top. Once he stopped and looked straight out to sea for a few minutes, long enough for Hopkins to break into the silence.

"What are you looking for?"

"I don't know. All I've got now are a lot of unanswered questions. What time is it?"

"Late."

"In more ways than one." Noonan was silent for a moment. He looked back down the bridge from the way they had come. Then he turned and looked the other way. When he had completed his visual tour on the street level, he stepped back and stared straight up at the beams vanishing into the ether above. Then he walked over and looked down into the waters 200 feet below.

Hopkins was about to break the silence when Noonan broke it for him. "What time does it get dark around here?"

"Well, it's two o'clock now. You've got another three hours of good light. Maybe even four, depending on what you call dark."

Noonan thought for a moment. "There's no reason for you to hang around with me anymore . . ." Hopkins was about to speak but Noonan waved him off. "I think I'm going to stay here on the bridge for a while. But if you would, use your cellular and have a motorcycle unit meet me somewhere along this side of the walkway. I don't know exactly where I'll be but initially, I'll be on this side. I'll also need a camera and a couple of rolls of film."

"Why not just use a cell phone?" Hopkins asked.

"First, I left mine in North Carolina. Second, photos from a cell phone are very poor quality."

"OK. An old fashioned camera and film."

"Add a roll of crime scene tape and a ruler. And I'll need a cell phone."

Hopkins started to hand Noonan his phone but Noonan shook his head. "No. Not yours. I need you to keep yours in case I want to get in touch with you."

"What are you planning on doing?" Hopkins asked as he wrote down what Noonan needed on the back of one of his business cards.

"Like I said before, I don't know."

Hopkins scribbled on the back of one of his business cards. "My home phone, cellular and fax numbers are listed here. I'll be available 24 hours for you."

"That won't be necessary. I work alone, or at least as alone as you can on any kind of an investigation. I don't want to sound rude but that's the way I work."

"Oh, that's all right, Captain. I'm at your disposal. Anything you need I'll be happy to provide."

"Good. Now, while I'm on the bridge, I'd like some documents. Do you have a few more business cards?"

"I've even got a piece of paper," Hopkins replied as he dug out a napkin for the Railroad Bar and Grill from his jacket pocket. "I never thought I'd be using this for a laundry list."

"You never know what you need until you need it."

Hopkins looked at him strangely. "That sounds like some kind of an old Polish proverb."

"You've been watching too much Banacek. Now, I need a rundown on the three people who had access to the vault. Second, I want a copy of the insurance report on the security for the bank. I also want all the documentation on the $10 million in cash. If the bank is less than two years old..."

"It is."

"...then I need a list of the original staff and, if there are any holdovers, people who are still employed there, I want those names. If any of those people have moved up and are now managers, vice presidents, or in upper management elsewhere in the Butterfield-Fargo system, I want those names too. Are you getting all of this?"

"I'm writing as fast as this napkin will let me."

"Good. Now I also want to know where the Greyhound bus was actually located before it was given to the perps and what kind of a homing device was put on the bus. Who put the device on the bus? Who was responsible for choosing the homing device and how well was he, or she, trained in the use of the device? Where was it placed on the structure of the bus? There's more so you'll have to turn the napkin over. Or re-fold it."

Hopkins maneuvered the napkin around and found a still-white area.

Noonan continued. "I'll also need a security check on everyone who had access to the video equipment on this bridge from today backward. For some reason those cameras didn't work. I'll bet if you search the cables you'll find splice or clamp marks. There was so much happening so fast I'll bet no one noticed before."

"I'll have them check whatever records they have."

"Good. Now I know this is quite a bit of work but this case is going to come to a head very quickly."

"What makes you think so?"

"There are still ten people missing and the bus hasn't turned up. Right now everyone who can put on a uniform is looking under every rock in San Francisco. We know the bus didn't cross the Golden Gate Bridge. Right now every Greyhound into and out of the city is being stopped and searched and after the press starts talking about the missing Greyhound..."

"They already have. They're calling it The Matter of the Vanishing Greyhound."

"Good. Good. This time the press is doing us a favor. We're going to find the missing bus fairly quickly. The hostages won't be on it but we'll find the bus. Then it's up to the lab people to find a clue. Right now we've got precious few."

"This is quite a list. Is that all?"

"For the moment, yeah. By the way, did anyone think to triangulate the cellular phone when the perp jumped online?"

"Yes we did think about it but no, we didn't think it would do any good. The perp was only on the line for about 15 minutes and we didn't even know he had a cell phone until the Greyhound took off. Most of the time he was on the phone he was moving. Worse, from our point of view, there are about a dozen cellular phone companies in San Francisco so we'd have to contact all of them – at midnight – to open their office and turn on their equipment."

"I see. I think that's enough for the moment."

"I hope so. I'll have as much of this documentation delivered to your hotel as soon as I can get it. St. Francis, right? I thought I heard the Chief say your luggage would be sent there."

Noonan nodded his head.

Hopkins put the napkin in his wallet and slid the wallet into the inside pocket of his jacket. "The information you want may come in a piece at a time but you should have all of it by midnight."

"By the way, when the perp called the Chief, did the message go to his private phone or through the main switchboard?"

"I don't know but I'll find out."

"How about the press? How did they get the story?"

"I don't know either but I'll try to find out. The press isn't too keen on revealing their sources."

"Who told you about the robbery?"

"I got the call from the Chief himself. Probably about 10:30 in the a.m. Right after he found out who the insurance agent was."

"Was the press there when you got to the bank?"

"Like ticks on a hound dog. I got there about 11:15."

Noonan grunted and stuck his hand forward. "It's been a pleasure. I'm sure we'll see each other again very soon. But, as I told you before, I work alone."

"I consider it an honor to be working with you at all, Captain. Anything I can do for you let me know."

"Well, as long as you can get me that information," Noonan pointed to the spot on Hopkins' jacket where he had stuffed the napkin into his pocket, "we'll be friends forever."

Chapter 3

Hopkins was still laughing as he pulled his cellular phone out of his jacket pocket. He waved as Noonan walked away from him, down the sidewalk of the bridge, heading for Sausalito.

Chapter 4

"What is our risk at this moment, Douglas?" The Regional Vice President for Pacific Rim Operations for English Petroleum, Robert Harrah, leaned forward on his elbows braced on his blotter. He was an ancient man; his features set in granite and soaked in pickle brine. "Let me reiterate what our arrangement with you is, Douglas. We pay you a considerable amount of money to make certain our cash transactions are discrete. We would have thought this would have been a fairly easy occupation. We deposit money in cash in a bank you insure, and you protect us from undue scrutiny."

"There is no risk here," Hopkins said quietly. "At the moment, there is no risk. There are just some complications."

"Complications?" Now we have what you lightly describe as complications. This is not acceptable, Mr. Hopkins."

If the lights had been turned up to their proper brilliance, the Harrah's office would have been stunning. Actually, stunning would hardly have been the word to describe the personal office of the highest placed individual outside the main office in Bristol. He was more than the embodiment of English Petroleum in the United States. He was English Petroleum in the United States. His was the face dominating every EP gasoline station across the United States, the pinched face of the British aristocrat stating he was so tight he squeaked and he always got his gas from EP because every penny counted. The second most well-known image EP presented to the United States was this man's pocket purse, brimming with pennies while, in the background, was the man's face pinched into a smile against the EP logo.

Chapter 4

The private persona of the man was on the other side of the universe. His office occupied the westward-facing one-third of the 123rd floor of the recently built EP building in San Francisco, referred to as the ENPET building by those who worked there and the block privy by those who worked for Atlantic Richfield, Exxon and Hastings-Hanford. Almost twice the height of the Bank of America Tower, ENPET stood as a giant shaft piercing the sky while the rest of the city's skyscrapers seemed nothing more than warts on the landscape below.

Harrah's desk was set on a massive dish in the center of his office. It rotated along a 180-degree arc once every hour thus offering him a different view of San Francisco every time he looked up. His massive teak desk dominated one-third of the office. Behind the desk and recessed into the cedar wall was a wet bar with a conference room beyond. Souvenirs of his peripatetic career and fortune loaded the shelves and walls of the conference room. Grip-and-grins from Saudi Arabia to Singapore covered one wall and on the other were spirit masks, blowguns, Tiki shields, rusty bronze Buddhas, and what had once been a 75-pound king salmon from Kachemak Bay in Alaska.

But on occasions such as this, the twin doors to the conference room were closed. Blinds covered the windows and the overhead light was turned down until the room seemed more like a cave than a business office. Rather than allowing the deep, rich luster of the cedar paneling to warm the room, the darkness turned the wood an ominous black with deeper black veins barely visible in the gloom. It was Kafkaesque.

"Well, since we are being so candid, allow me to refresh your memory as to our relationship." Hopkins took a drag on his cigarette and let the smoke waterfall out of his mouth. "You are paying me, and quite well I must add, to make certain your cash transactions are secure and covered with insurance. Upon occasion, nicely put, I am paid to make certain all the serial numbers of those actual bills are scrambled. I have not failed you."

Harrah was unimpressed. "True. But the problem we have here, Douglas, is not just the $10 million of our money which is at risk. The actual cash, which was in the bank, places us at risk because we don't have a list of those serial numbers. What should have been a sleight-of-hand transaction has turned into a full-blown disaster. There are now 10 hostages at risk threatening to turn what should have been a simple bank robbery into a national hurricane of concern. Captain Noonan of the Sandersonville Police, probably the highest profile crime fighter in America, is in San

Francisco. Then there's the question of the contents of the safety deposit boxes. What we have here, Douglas, is a full-fledged public relations and fiscal disaster about to explode like an atom bomb. We cannot afford any scrutiny, Mr. Hopkins, and neither can you."

"True, Robert, but let me remind you it was on your instruction the money was to be placed in that particular bank for laundering..."

"Not laundering, Mr. Hopkins."

"Whatever verb you use is fine with me, Mr. Harrah, but let's be frank. The problem here is your money just happened to be in a bank which was hit. Your paperwork is good and your cash is insured. Whatever happens, you get $10 million back."

"That's not the point, Mr. Hopkins. The point is we do not want the scrutiny this robbery could be causing us. We want the money which was in the bank back."

This clearly took Hopkins by surprise. He stalled mid-stab with his cigarette hovering over the ashtray on Harrah's desk. "You want the money that was in the bank back?" he said with incredulity. "You mean you want the exact dollars back? The same bills?"

"That's right."

Hopkins sat in stunned silence for a moment. "First of all, why? You're covered for the $10 million."

"Because we are very nervous about having the IRS find out we've been playing fast and loose with cash. It makes them nervous even though it is legal and because we don't need any undue attention from the IRS."

"What's the problem? If any of the serial numbers of the original bills show up in circulation, you can say it was part of the robbery. They don't have the replacement serial numbers so, as I asked before, what is the problem?"

Harrah stood up and slowly walked to the window where he crushed a button in the window frame as though it was a bug. Along the entire wall the blinds flipped up. Normally these blinds were operated by small motors which adjusted the amount of light allowed into the office. With the button he could override the system. When the blinds were raised entirely, he stood before the window and looked at his kingdom below. Without turning he continued to talk to Hopkins.

"Well, we at English Petroleum are concerned the new serial numbers on the bills will come back to haunt us. Someone might be able to get their hands on the original list of serial numbers which were recorded with the IRS and prove the bills which were stolen were not the same serial numbers. Then English Petroleum might be asked to pay a pretty penny to keep such information, shall we say, proprietary."

"But only two or three people even know our little secret."

"Precisely. We intend to keep it that way. So we'll solve our little problem right now. We want the original $10 million back. Do I make myself clear?"

"How am I supposed to arrange that?"

"Bluntly stated, Mr. Hopkins, I don't care. You clearly arranged the robbery so you should know where the money is located."

"Look," Hopkins was now breaking into a sweat, "I didn't have anything to do with the bank robbery. It just happened. I don't know who those thieves are. I don't know where the money is. I don't know how to reach them."

"Oh, that is such a pity, Mr. Hopkins." Harrah began raising the other blinds and looking down into the streets of San Francisco in the deep cement canyons below. From where Hopkins sat, the effect was to outline Harrah against the early morning light. "Mr. Hopkins, today is going to be a very difficult day. It is now 7:15 and in 45 minutes I'm going to have to go into a large, unfriendly meeting and tell some very influential men a critical component to a multi-trillion dollar negotiation is in jeopardy because you, Mr. Hopkins, failed to protect our assets and the integrity of our operating system, a task which you were well paid to perform."

"Hey, it's not my fault…"

"Fault is not the question here. Responsibility is. The gentlemen and lady with whom I will be meeting will be very displeased with the state of this matter. They do not view failure as an option. You have been paid well and you will be expected to maintain your end of the bargain."

"But I don't know where to find those dollars! I had nothing to do with the robbery!"

"Oh, I hope you are lying, Mr. Hopkins. I truly do. Because if the $10 million which disappeared, the same $10 million let me reiterate, is not within our possession by midnight tomorrow, you will not see the sun rise again. Do I make myself clear?" Harrah sat behind his massive desk deftly.

"You can't just go around and make threats like…" Hopkins words came so close to the heels of Harrah's they seemed like one run-on sentence.

"Yes I can. The mechanism is already in place and no one is going to let any individual stand in the way of a multi-trillion operation, not me and certainly not you."

"But how are you going to get the exact $10 million if I'm out of the picture."

"We may not. But if we cannot and any irregularities are found, we will leave the blame with you. Under the circumstances you won't be able to dispute the charges, eh? It also solves the problem of having you return in a year for a readjustment of your commission rate with us, if you know what I mean."

"You're saying you think I'm going to blackmail you."

"Blackmail is such a nasty word. I prefer the American vernacular, shakedown."

"Even if you think that – which isn't true – you can't just go out and kill someone! This is the United States, for God's sake."

Harrah's voice was smooth and contained, just as though he were ordering a kidney potpie or a stout. "Oh, yes we can. And we will. You have made a mess of the matter and at a critical moment. I would strongly suggest you do everything in your power to retrieve the original $10 million, particularly if Captain Noonan is on the case. I doubt he will be as foolish as you have been."

"But I really don't know who the thieves are!" Hopkins said plaintively but his voice was hollow of sincerity.

"Then you had better find out at once, don't you think?"

There was silence in the room for a long moment as Harrah went back to his office chair. Hopkins was in a leather chair almost quivering while Harrah looked down on the insurance agent as if he were a rabbit skittering along an open meadow with a bald eagle dropping out of the sky.

"Now, Douglas. Look at me, Douglas."

Hopkins shifted his gaze until he was looking into the coldest eyes he had ever seen. It was clear from the expression on his face there was not a doubt in his mind the president of English Petroleum would be true to his word.

"Good. Now, Douglas. Let me tell you what I think. I think you planned this entire operation. You and your cohorts got the $10 million and your company covers the loss. Very clever if I do say so myself – and I do – but I don't think you were stupid enough to tell your associates the bills were untraceable. If you had we wouldn't be talking right now. You and your friends would be gone. No, there is something else holding you in town."

"Well . . ." Hopkins started to speak but Harrah cut him with an imperial wave of his hand. "I'm going to make your job incredibly easy for you,

Douglas. Through your connections, whatever they are, I expect you to find the men who pulled off this job and let them know you want the original $10 million back in our hands by midnight tomorrow. You'll have to make your own arrangements but I want those bills back in my possession by midnight tomorrow. And you may also pass along to the thieves if even a single $100 bill makes it into circulation I will make certain everyone associated with this robbery is hunted down and disposed of with."

"You, you can't do that!"

"Douglas, English Petroleum is not a sovereign nation. It is a company with vast holdings and connections all over the world. In many countries we deal with very unsavory individuals who are more than willing to perform, shall we say, unusual tasks. No matter where those men go, we will find them and we will eliminate them. Now," Harrah leaned back comfortably in his office chair. "There's no reason for this matter to have an unpleasant ending. You just find the thieves, deliver my message clearly and I'm sure we can reach an accommodation."

Harrah rose indicating the conversation was at an end. Hopkins, almost blubbering, rose slowly.

"Once again, let me make myself crystal clear," Harrah walked ahead of Hopkins leading him toward the elevator. "If the original $10 million from the bank is not replaced before midnight tomorrow then you will not see the morning sun. And your associates will not be far behind. Melodramatic this may sound but true it is." The last was said with finality and Harrah, with an outstretched hand toward his private elevator, indicated the meeting was over. Hopkins tried to say something but Harrah just looked at him and said a single word, "Midnight."

There was a moment of silence before the elevator clicked shut and Hopkins was shot down to the street level. Only after he had been gone a full 30 seconds did the door to the conference room open and two men emerge from the semi-darkness.

The two men were as similar as a python and a hedgehog. The taller was a cadaverous, six-foot specimen who would have appeared more at home in a black oak coffin than a business office. His suit hung on him rather than fit and his nose was sharp enough to cut cheese.

The other man was built like the Tasmanian Devil of Walt Disney fame. His corpulent body stretched his suit whenever he moved yet, at the same time, his legs were so spindly his trouser legs appeared empty. Despite his body's proportions, he moved with agility, like a dancer on stage.

The Matter of the Vanishing Greyhound

"You heard?" Harrah didn't offer either man a chair but they sat, nonetheless.

"All of it," the taller man said laconically.

"What a piker," said the fat man as he put the heel of his right palm on the desk for support as he sat. "He thinks $10 million is a fortune. He's lying,"

"I believe so, yes." Harrah leaned back against the dark wall next to the elevator. "And I believe even if he succeeds we cannot count on his loyalty."

"Or his silence." The taller man looked to the fat man for confirmation. The fat man was silent.

There was a long moment of silence which was only broken when Harrah pushed himself away from the wall. "Give him until about 11 p.m. tomorrow. If it doesn't look like he's going to find the money, take him out. If he's close, let him be."

"And if he succeeds?" The fat man asked the question as if it were rhetorical.

"We have seven trillion dollars riding on an insurance agent who got greedy. First time failure is last time risk. Take him out."

"And his associates?" The fat man smiled and patted the front of his suit at the waistline.

"Not here. Not now. But things could change."

There was a moment of silence. Both men rose and walked to the elevator. The fat man pushed the button. When the door popped open, the two men stepped aboard and the elevator closed. Harrah, alone, walked back to the window to look down on San Francisco. It was going to be a very long day, he thought. A very long day.

Chapter 5

Candice Greenleaf, Branch Manager and Chief Teller Supervisor of the Butterfield-Fargo First Bank of San Francisco, awoke to melodious music wafting through the speakers set flush against the sheetrock walls of the room. For a moment she lay quietly on the cot, her eyes adjusting to the darkness. Then, slowly, the lights came up. When it became too bright to be comfortable, she pulled back the rough army blanket and pulled herself slowly to a seated position. All around her, the nine other employees of the Butterfield-Fargo First National Bank were beginning to stir, everyone on his or her cot and each covered with an identical gray-brown army blanket.

To the untrained eye, the room looked like a cube with five of the six planes covered with sheetrock and the sixth side, the floor, was a flat sea of particleboard.

To the trained eye it looked the same.

A bank of florescent lights was inset into the ceiling a dozen feet off the floor and twin video cameras on opposite walls surveyed the ten hostages with nary a blink. In addition to several ventilation grates, somewhere in the ceiling were some microphones, possibly in the light trenches. They had to be there, the hostages had agreed previously, because no one could spot them anywhere else.

Particularly stressing was the fact no one had been able to spot any sprinkler system in the ceiling, a fact which condemned the three smokers in the group into a fit of panic which was only alleviated when it was agreed they be allowed to smoke in the shower stall only. The butts were submerged in a coffee can half-filled with water and kept in the bathroom to cut down on the possibility of a fire.

The hostages actually occupied two rooms; three if one were to count the entryway. The main room was 100 feet long by 20 feet wide, paced for accurate measurement the first hour the hostages had been incarcerated. Ten cots with futon padding and army blankets were scattered about at one end of the room. A weight machine, three tables along with a dozen chairs dominated the other end of the enclosure. Piles of magazines, comic books, mystery novels and crossword puzzle books were scattered around the tables like flotsam around a pier at slack tide. An ongoing game of Monopoly was in play on the red card table, one of the players clearly about to foreclose on everyone else, and, on the two six-foot-long institutional Formica models, a jigsaw puzzle was painfully being assembled and a poker game, complete with Caesar's Palace chips, had a sizable pot waiting for one of the last three of the original five in the game. In the back corner, by the bathroom door, were two large metal frames each holding an oversized, black, polyethylene garbage bag. Both bags were half-filled.

Set into the wall beside the garbage bag frames was the door to the bathroom. It was an institutional establishment with three toilets set along one wall followed by three washbasins over a tile floor. In the corner of the room was a GI-issue metal table piled with toilet paper rolls, feminine sanitary products, facial tissue, spray deodorants, toothbrushes in boxes and toothpaste. There were also some hairdryers and make-up kits. A military-style shower stall dominated the back of the bathroom like a walk-in closet with piles of white locker room towels on shelving. A third polyethylene bag, this one for wet towels, was in a frame in the bathroom.

"Good morning, my friends, good morning." It was the cheery voice of John, the name their captor had christened himself. "It's another typical San Francisco day, my friends. A bit cold, in the mid-60s according to the weather people. The fog is expected to blow off so it should be clear. I'm sorry you are going to miss the stunning view today."

"We're sorry too," shouted Greenleaf and three of the other hostages clapped weakly from their cots.

"I know how you feel; I really do," replied John. "Your stay here is an inconvenience for both you and me, believe me. Now, you know the routine. If you place all of your garbage bags in the entryway, I'll see you get a nice warm breakfast. As you requested, this morning it is from Burger King."

Chapter 5

The room erupted with moans and razzing.

"I'm sorry but it's the best I can do for the moment. But you may be pleased to know this is probably your last night here in the box. Everything seems to be moving along well in the outside world. If it continues to move along as well as we anticipate, there is every reason to believe you will be home in your own beds by midnight. Won't it be lovely?"

"Up yours!" one of the tellers shrieked. Someone else gave John a raspberry.

"Not nice, not nice," John responded. "But I understand. I do have a special treat for you this morning. I'll give you a dozen copies of today's newspaper so you can read all about our exploits. As you can see, we are quite modest. You may find it interesting the police believe you have been taken out of the San Francisco area because a large-scale manhunt has failed to find the bus." The voice paused for a moment, "or you. Such a pity."

Greenleaf shook her head clear and let her feet feel around for the floor for her shoes. She should have known better. As soon as the big toe on her right found the particleboard, she picked up a splinter. She snapped her foot back and then leaned over to pick up her shoes by hand. Overhead, John droned on.

"It's going to be a long day for all of us so make sure you are fresh and ready to travel. It's a little after seven in the morning and we expect to be moving by ten so you will have three hours to tidy up and make ready to go."

As soon as John signed off, there was a hubbub of grumbling. No one was interested in staying where they were but no one seemed willing to take the chance they weren't going to be killed.

The youngest teller, Cheri Molk, a temporary who had the misfortune to have been assigned to the bank the morning of the robbery pulled Greenleaf aside. "Do you really think they're going to let us go? I mean, my luck so far has been bad."

"The good news, Cheri, we haven't seen anyone's face. At the very least it means the bad guys are trying to make sure we don't know who they are. The bad news is there had to have been an inside person on this job."

"Really?"

"There are only three people who could have been the inside person – and two of them are in here with us."

"Really?"

55

"Yeah. The man who's been wearing the bow tie and the woman in the gray-and-black suit. Or what was a suit before we started on this trip. Be very careful what you say around those two."

"Really?"

Greenleaf leaned over as she slipped her shoes on. As she was bent over she leaned toward the young teller and said softly, "Give me another of those deposit slips, Cheri. It's a good thing you kept those from your interview for this job."

"Really?"

Molk dug around in the jacket of her dark blue jersey which was folded on a chair at the head of the cot.

"Don't flash those around, Cheri. You never know who's watching." Molk handed her the pack of deposit slips.

"We've got five left. We left one in the bus, one in the truck and I'm going to leave another one here. You never know who'll find one of these." Greenleaf surreptitiously waved one of the Butterfield-Fargo First National deposit slips as she slipped it between the rough futon and the canvas of the camp cot. "Maybe it'll help someone find us."

"Really?"

"Yes, really."

Chapter 6

It had been a short night for Captain Heinz Noonan. He had been on the Golden Gate with the lab team until well after the sun went down. Then he was up until midnight pouring over the paperwork he had requested. He was down for a short night, but it gave him no rest and he awoke unrested and restless.

Early.

He didn't need the wake-up call for 7 a.m. Already up and moving by 6:30 a.m., he placed a person-to-person call to his assistant in Sandersonville and discovered a suitcase full of his working clothes and equipment had been left in the early afternoon the day before. He traced the suitcase to the hotel lobby where it was waiting for him downstairs. By the time he did receive the automated call telling him it was 7 a.m., he was dressed in his traditional working clothing: black field boots, khaki pants, and teal shirt with an open collar. His trademark black leather jacket had come to San Francisco on the plane with him.

The moment he looked out his window it was clear today and was not going to be the same as yesterday. It looked like Sandersonville. There was a low-hanging fog bank with what appeared to be blowing mist near the ground. Automobiles were picking their way through the pea soup, pedestrians were trying to decide if they wanted their umbrellas up or down and no one was worrying about a suntan. Noonan popped the window open and took a deep lungful of the cold marine air.

"My kind of weather," he mumbled to himself. "You don't get sunburn; you just rust."

The Matter of the Vanishing Greyhound

After he placed a call to Chief Thayer he began pawing through the suitcase which had been sent from his office. He pulled out his tape measure, pocket knife, magnifying glass, some mechanical pencils and a small notebook. He took a handful of plastic bags and stuffed them in his hip pocket. Finally, after he dug around in the suitcase for a good three minutes, he pulled a small penlight out of the bag. He unscrewed the cap and dropped the batteries in his hand. Since they were reversed for safety, he placed them into the flashlight body correctly and screwed the light back in place. The light flashed when he hit the switch and he grunted with satisfaction.

Downstairs in the lobby, the Chief was waiting for him. The first thing he handed Noonan was a cup of coffee in a green and yellow paper cup. At the same time, he beckoned Noonan out the door with his arm. On the run, they made it through the rotating door of the hotel and headed across the wet sidewalk to the Chief's car.

"I hope you don't mind eating on the run, or at least not right now."

"To serve and protect, George, my reason for being here."

"Not unless you're in Los Angeles. This is San Francisco, remember."

"Yeah, where little cable cars climb halfway to the stars, what surprises do you have for me today?"

"I'm feeling great after nine hours of sleep. You didn't get that much. How're you feeling?"

"Fine. I was up 'til midnight going over paperwork. Did you have some lab reports for me?"

The Chief opened the passenger door to the car and indicated the envelope on the passenger seat. Noonan got in and pulled the door closed as the Chief scampered around the squad car and slid in behind the wheel. The car was in gear, out of the loading zone, and into traffic before Noonan had the envelope open.

As soon as the car began to gain speed, the Chief dug a cellular phone out of his jacket pocket. He handed it to Noonan back first so he could see the list of cellular numbers taped the back of the phone.

"While I was asleep you were a busy boy," the Chief said. "You walked our bridge from end to end. Not a lot of San Franciscans have done that. As you can see from those reports, our lab people worked all night."

"Good," Noonan replied as he pulled out the staples with his fingernails. "I need all the information I can get as soon as I can get it."

"But," the Chief sighed, "they don't have much to tell you. They went over the three places on the top of the fence you marked off but all they found were scrapes and scratches on two of them. The third had two different kinds of paint, a light gray and black. The one place on the support strut you wanted examined showed some nylon fibers but nothing else."

"I kind of thought it would."

"What's the secret, Heinz? Do you really think the paint and the nylon fibers have something to do with the robbery? The spot is a half-mile past the three bungee cords!"

"George, what I can't do is duplicate what your people are doing. If they could have found the hostages and money by now, you wouldn't need me. The advantage I bring you is I don't think like a normal policeman, if there is such a thing as a normal policeman. All of the perps I deal with, the tough cases anyway, operate effectively because they know how the police think. They count on the police operating by the book. The police are very obliging when it comes to operating by the book. So the perps benefit. It's like betting on clockwork."

"Isn't that a little simplified?"

"No. Not really. If you have 25 police officers in a room and every one of them has a college degree in psychology or police science, when you present them with a problem, they are all going to approach the problem with the same point of view. It's what they learned in school; it's how they've been trained to think and all the way through their career, they're expected to think like a cop. In reality, all cops think alike. But if you really want to see a police department flower, get yourself recruits who have degrees in music, biology, mathematics, physics, or art. You get crossfertilization of thinking when you have cops who have different backgrounds, different degrees and different life experiences."

"What did you get your degree in, Heinz?"

"European history and anthropology. Not a very promising start for a police career, eh?"

"Yeah. How did you get into police work?"

"Too long a story to go into now." Noonan slid the pile of lab reports back into the envelope on his lap. "Right now we've got ten hostages to find. How has the press been treating us?"

The Chief grunted and reached over the back seat to pick up a Wednesday paper off the back seat. He tossed it onto Noonan's lap. "As good as can be expected. The nice thing about the press is they're polite. There are a couple of cowboys out sniffing around but by and large they're leaving us to do our job."

The Matter of the Vanishing Greyhound

Noonan nodded in agreement as he looked over the stories in the paper. "They're polite right now because there's no way they can dig around for clues in places you haven't been. Give them another 24 hours and they'll be scouring the city for hostages. The first impulse of the press is to go sensational, interview tearful families and neighbors."

"Then they are operating true to form."

"Good, it'll keep the bad guys busy for a few more hours, long enough for us to wrap this up." Noonan smiled.

"You think you can wrap this up today?" The Chief was clearly fishing for a positive response.

"Should be able to."

"The other bit of immediate news is the FBI has arrived. As soon as the clock hit 24 hours, two agents in polyester showed up and said they were in charge."

Noonan snorted. "Dunkin' Donuts will be happy. Do you have any more good news?"

Early morning traffic in San Francisco looked just about like afternoon traffic. The only difference was drivers were asleep at the wheel rather than suffering from 9-to-5 burnout. There was a constant rumble of vehicle tires drumming on streets whose surface varied from block to block: cobblestone to black top to pothole-strewn-cement to brick. There was an occasional plaintive bleep of a horn but the most distinctive sound was of buses accelerating away from a curb only to decelerate in the next block for another plug of passengers. If BART was supposed to have reduced the number of passengers on the surface transportation network, there was no indication it was working.

"Yes, as a matter of fact," the Chief said as he looked over his left shoulder before he pulled into an intersection to slide through a left hand turn. "I do have some good news. While we were both asleep the bus turned up. Unfortunately I'm not sure how much information we can get from it."

"Where was it found?"

"The best place to hide something is in plain sight and that's where it was. The bus turned up at the Greyhound bus yard."

"It was just sitting there?"

"Yup. The perps had changed the license plates on the bus and then left it sitting in the to-be-cleaned area. When a bus trip terminates, the vehicle is washed on the outside and cleaned on the inside. The perps drove the Greyhound into the washing yard early in the morning the day after the bus disappeared. They switched the plates with another bus and our bus went through a cleaning. They only discovered the switch when they spotted the other bus whose plates had been switched. It was parked in a set of nine buses, too deep to be used until last night. Someone spotted the plates and discovered the switch."

"Any chance of getting what was taken off the bus?"

"My people were on it right away. They dug through a dumpster and found a small bag from our stolen bus. There's not much there. It appears our perps cleaned out the bus thoroughly. The only thing of interest was this," the Chief said as he pulled a plastic bag from the inside pocket of his jacket. He handed it to Noonan who recognized it as a bank deposit slip from Butterfield-Fargo First National.

"Good link for us but I don't think it's too important." Noonan handed the slip in the plastic bag back to the Chief. "But it does show someone is thinking."

"That's what we thought too."

Noonan tipped the paper coffee cup back and took his first sip of the black liquid. When he tilted the cup back, steam vented through the small drinking hole and coated his glasses.

"Was anything else of interest found in the bus?"

"Nope. Apparently it was pretty clean when it was put through the washing system. I'm assuming you wanted to see the bus. We're going there now."

"Good."

"How about the material I sent over last night. Did you find anything important in the paperwork?"

"I don't know. My style of investigation involves looking over lots and lots of documents and then seeing what pops out as time goes along. I call it 'massing the trivia.' I won't know what's important and what's garbage until the case is over."

"I hope this all wraps up quickly, I've got heat from above, the paper's been nipping at my heels and there are ten sets of relatives screaming for action. I've got nothing but an empty bus and $10 million in cash missing – not to mention what was in those safety deposit boxes."

"Be thankful the perps haven't tried to ransom the hostages." The Chief laughed sadly.

If Noonan expected the Greyhound to reveal any secrets, he was doomed to disappointment. It sat in a corner of the wash down area with

The Matter of the Vanishing Greyhound

a police guard wandering about in the early morning fog. A bright yellow police tape was tacked to the cyclone fence and stretched to a stone on the ground and then to a patrol car before reaching back to the cyclone fence in front of the bus.

As the Chief had indicated, there wasn't much to see. Noonan spent a few minutes on his back in the bus looking under the seats with his flashlight but couldn't find anything of interest. He dug through the small bag of garbage, which had been collected from the bus but again, found nothing of merit. The homing device which had been installed by the police was gone.

"They've been a step ahead of us all the way." The Chief ran his finger over the spot where the homing device had been hidden in the front wheel well.

"Maybe not," Noonan replied. "A simple homing device detection would have told them where the bug was on the bus. They could have bought the device at any one of a dozen retail stores in town."

Noonan washed his hands in the Greyhound terminal restroom and then he was back in the patrol car heading across town.

"The only other place I could think you would want to visit is English Petroleum to talk to them about their money."

"You know how I think. Yes, thanks. I don't know how productive a visit would be but let's give it a shot."

"We have an appointment with the Regional Vice President for Pacific Rim Operations, Robert Harrah . ."

"The British pinch penny, right?"

"Same guy. He's very personable and not anything like his TV persona. He's said he'll make time for us whenever we show up. I figured you'd want to talk with him as soon as possible. Afterwards, we can have breakfast. Then the rest of the day is yours."

"Good." Noonan smoothed his beard with his hand. "This is going to be a very interesting conversation."

He was right.

It was also a very short conversation.

If nothing else, Harrah was unexpectedly cultured and polite, which was quite a switch from what Noonan clearly expected him to be. Noonan commented on that and Harrah laughed, "It's all in the presentation, Captain. The magic of the tele. Won't you sit down?" He indicated two carved teak chairs in front of his desk, "Please."

Chapter 6

Noonan unbuttoned his leather jacket and sat cross-legged. "I'll come right to the point, Mr. Harrah, in addition to the ten hostages there's also $10 million in cash which belongs to English Petroleum. At the risk of being rude because of the time crunch, why is English Petroleum keeping so much money available in cash?"

"I understand your position perfectly, Captain, and being abrupt under the circumstances is not out of line, as you chaps say over here. However, I'm not at liberty to say why the money is being kept in cash," Harrah giving a Cheshire cat grin. "While I can assure you it is perfectly legal for us to do so, I appreciate you are looking for any lead to find those ten hostages." As he was speaking he opened the top drawer of his desk and pulled out a legal-sized envelope. "Anticipating your questions, I have had our legal department provide as much information as they..."

Noonan tried to butt in. "But I am still very interested in knowing the purpose for the $10 million in cash. I don't care what the reason is, it may provide me..." Noonan was unsuccessful.

He was cut off as Harrah handed him the envelope.

"Also included in this packet is an indication from the IRS stating they are well aware of our practice of keeping millions of dollars in cash available for exigencies."

"The bottom line," Noonan tried again, "as I take it, is this is all the help we can expect from English Petroleum?" Noonan casually jiggled the envelope at eye level.

"Captain! We are every bit as concerned over the fate of those ten hostages as you are! Perhaps even more so. According to the newspaper, the reason the thieves chose that particular bank was because of the $10 million in cash. That makes us very responsible in the public eye. We want those thieves caught as badly as you, perhaps more so because we have our good name at risk. Revenues from EP stations in California alone run well into the hundreds of millions. The faster those thieves are caught, the sooner things can go back to normal."

"I see." Noonan rose and the Chief followed suit a split-second later.

Harrah stood only after he pulled a business card out of the corner of his blotter. "This is the card of our Public Affairs Director," he said as he handed Noonan the card. "I also had him place his home phone and cellular number on the card. He has been given strict instruction to provide you with any information or assistance you want, day or night."

Noonan took the card and glanced at it, "except as to the purpose of the $10 million."

"He doesn't know," responded Harrah. "Only three of us in the United States do."

"Are you one of them?" Noonan asked.

Harrah was about to respond but changed his mind. He simply stuck his hand across the desk in Noonan's direction. "It's been a pleasure, Captain. Chief. Always a pleasure."

Two minutes later Noonan and the Chief were on their way down the elevator to Market Street.

"Hardly worth the effort was it?" snapped Noonan as he pulled his seat belt across his chest. "The nicest brush-off I've ever received."

The Chief shook his head. "English Petroleum is one of those old stuffy English corporations which believes United States should still be a colony. Their attitude is they are here to do business, not make friends. If it wasn't for their ad campaign, they wouldn't be making a dime on the West Coast."

"The power of television," Noonan responded as he put down the envelope. "Basically what he gave us is diddly. In essence, the paperwork says their insurance agent Douglas Hopkins was responsible for everything, talk to him. We at English Petroleum are pure as the driven snow."

"Did you expect anything different?"

"Frankly, yes." Noonan smiled sadly. "What I got was nothing more than the contempt of a colonial governor for the natives."

"Welcome to life in a debtor nation."

Chapter 7

If nothing else, the perps were prompt. Just as John had said they would be moved at 10 a.m., almost to the second the panel truck with the ten seats bolted in the rear backed up to the entryway of the room where the hostages were being held. For the second time in two days, Candice Greenleaf and the other nine hostages were hustled aboard the truck. A canvas sheet had been tossed over the truck to disguise its appearance and license plate, a fact Cheri Molk was quick to point out to Greenleaf. Greenleaf just nodded her head and sat down in the same seat she had taken the first night when they had been hustled out of the Greyhound bus in a dark warehouse. She sat down and on the cold, green, plastic make-shift chair and attached the seat belt, which had been bolted to the wooden wall of the truck. It was the same seat she had been in the previous night. When the latch was closed, she let her hand wander down the side of the chair and underneath. There her fingers came in contact with the Butterfield-Fargo deposit slip she had left there the night before. Then she set her hands on her lap and waited.

When all the passengers were in their seats, a fact confirmed by a perp who was obviously watching through a one-way mirror in the front wall of the panel truck, the van was closed with a sliding door. They could hear the latch catch and a lock secure the handle from the outside.

"There's no reason to worry, my friends," came the soothing voice of John over the intercom into the back of the truck. "There was a little complication which we are resolving. We're going to a new location. The trip should take about 15 minutes. As long as you behave yourself there won't be any problems. If there are, as I mentioned the last time you were in this van, we have attached some gas to make you immobile. So, just sit back and relax."

"Why do you think they're moving us?" asked the young teller as the truck lurched sideways as though it was bouncing through a field of potholes. Then it rolled onto the smooth pavement like a city street.

"As long as they're moving us, be happy. It's when they don't care about us we'll be in real trouble."

Chapter 8

Noonan would have opted to rent a car and drive himself, but when it was pointed out he didn't know his way around San Francisco, he settled for an unmarked car with a detective in plain clothes. The Chief pulled a detective out of the morning's lineup and Noonan had his escort. Hopkins offered to drive him around but Noonan turned him down. It was a polite turn down and if Hopkins took offense it wasn't obvious. Noonan waited until Hopkins pulled out of the parking lot at the police station and disappeared into traffic before he turned to the detective.

"Where to first, sir?"

Detective Smith was perfect for undercover work. She was one of those people who could fade into a crowd because she was nondescript. She was no taller than 5 feet 6 inches and was about 130 pounds. She was probably shorter because she was wearing padded black shoes, made for running after perps in comfort. There wasn't any flab on her frame and her uniform fit well but not so well as if it had been tailored. She had jet black straight hair, clearly part of her Native American heritage, and she was still at the age where she could advance her looks by a decade – or reduce it – with the right make-up. She had sharp black eyes and a clear complexion.

"Smith?" said Noonan with a question in his voice. "I hate to put it this way but you don't look like a Smith."

She laughed. "It's my ex-husband's name. A long time ago and far away. It was easier to keep his name than change all the credit cards. He wasn't a bad guy so I just kept the name. Do you want to know what my maiden name was, sir?"

The Matter of the Vanishing Greyhound

"Nope," Noonan replied with a smile. "Just don't call me sir. Heinz will do just fine."

"OK, Heinz. Where do we go from here?"

"Let's go to the Greyhound bus depot. I need some breakfast." Smith gave him a quizzical look.

Noonan smiled. "I want to talk with personnel there. As you drive I'll tell you what's been going on. By the way, what do you want me call you?"

"Smith is fine, si. . .," she almost got the sir out before she switched to "Heinz."

"That's right. Heinz. Just like the ketchup."

Breakfast was the usual fare for a Greyhound bus station: over-cooked, over-greased and over-priced. Smith settled for toast and coffee while Noonan had a mushroom omelet and home fries while the yard manager repeated how the Greyhound had been chosen and used in the hostage transport."

"We just pulled one out of the yard. It was the luck of the draw. The police said they wanted a bus pronto so we provided."

"Was there anything unusual about that bus?" Noonan looked over the photos of the bus he had from the lab team.

"The only thing unusual about that bus was it was used in a getaway. Like I told the police, we didn't even know it was back until it was washed and sanitized. Hey, if we hadn't moved those three buses in the back lot and spotted the plates, the police would still be searching San Francisco for number 854."

"Is there any reason for a bus to smoke?"

"Not the way the police were talking about. We went over 854 very carefully when we finally located it. Nope. Nothing wrong with the bus. Exhaust system was working AOK."

"AOK? No sign of tampering?"

"Not a one."

"Thanks." Noonan rose and Smith followed. Noonan picked up his tab, which was immediately grabbed by Smith and then snatched by the yard manager. "You just find the boys who used our bus for a heist. Besides, with the newspapers talking about the Vanishing Greyhound, it is the best publicity we've had for years."

The next stop was the Police Department.

"Why didn't we make this stop first?" Smith asked puzzled. "There's a heck of a better snack bar downstairs."

Chapter 8

"Ever go fishing?"
"Yeah."
"Do you catch any fish while everybody's standing on the bank talking?"
"I never thought about it that way."
"Well, the best time to go fishing is when it's real quiet."
"I get your point, Heinz. Where do you want to go?"
"To the office handling homing devices."
"You mean Property. Upstairs." Smith pointed up the stairs.

There was only a secretary in Property and her name tag identified her as an administrative assistant. There wasn't a name on her tag, just the indication she was the administrative assistant. She was a shade under 25 years of age and this was probably her first job. Or she was just nervous about all the attention because of the Vanishing Greyhound. So she was reluctant to open any files for a bearded man in his sixties from a police department she had never heard of even though he was accompanied by a plainclothes detective from San Francisco. Rules were rules.

"I'll have to have authorization to show you any files," she said and let a long pause go by before she said, "sir."

"Not a problem," Noonan replied, even before she finished her long pause. Then he pulled out his cellular phone and tapped in the Chief's number for speed dial. Ten seconds later, he and Smith were pouring over the paperwork for the night of the robbery.

"You know these forms better than I do," Noonan said to Smith. "The way I read it a homing device was checked out at, what, 11 p.m.?"

"You're reading the paperwork correctly."

"It was never returned, destroyed, lost. Is there any paperwork to indicate when a homing device was never returned?"

"Captain, we have forms for everything including how to fill out forms. There's a Form 12-98-054 for destroyed or lost property but it has to be over a certain dollar amount. Like $200. I don't know how much those homing devices cost but there wouldn't be a form for a missing device, this one for instance, because it isn't officially missing yet."

"When would it be officially missing?"

"When the case closes, I imagine."

"Fine. Now, the homing device that was used, when was it purchased?"

"It's a standard model for police departments. It could have been purchased three days before the robbery or three years ago. There's no secret about what kind of homing device we use. Anyone who knows where to

69

buy security equipment could order a homing device. They can even buy them here in San Francisco. There are three or four equipment retailers not counting the private security companies who probably have them on their shelves."

"Is there any way the perps could have known what kind of a homing device was being used by the San Francisco Police?"

"Oh, there's no question they knew we use homing devices and what kind. But the trick is, how did they know what frequency we were using? There are lots of homing devices out there on the street, but it's the frequency that makes a difference."

"How is the frequency set?"

"The factory does it. To get our frequency, they'd have to have gotten ahold of a homing device from right here. We turn it on here and then track it from here."

Noonan looked around the room. With the exception of the administrative assistant, the office was empty. "From where do you actually track it?"

Smith went over to a computer and flicked it on. When the screen jumped to life with a pop, she tapped in a password and the word PROPERTY AUTHORIZATION REQUIRED appeared on the screen.

"Anyone can get onto the police network but it will take a password to get into the Property hard drive. The password is changed frequently to keep the material secure."

"So the tracking of the bus had to be done from here?"

"I don't know if it had to be done from here but it was done from here. I used to work in Property so I know how it was done. It's quite simple, in fact. The homing device is activated and shows up on a computer template."

"You mean like on a map of the city?"

"Sort of. It's not as sophisticated as what you see in a James Bond movie. But it isn't as primitive as those World War II movies where the Nazis have to triangulate the position of a clandestine radio station."

"So keeping an eye on the homing device isn't difficult."

"No."

"What happens if there are three or four bugs out there at the same time? How can you keep from being confused as to who is carrying which bug?"

"Usually that's not a problem. You can change the frequency of each bug slightly so you can identify which bug is which if they are close together. Or you just make a template for each bug."

"You mean like a different computer screen for each bug?"

"Sort of. You know how you can have three or four documents up in a computer open at any one time but there is only one of those documents on the screen?"

"Multi-tasking."

"Right. You can do that with a homing computer too."

"So it would be possible to be looking at template 1 and not see the active homing devices on template 2 or 3."

"Yeah. If there were templates 2 and 3. Usually there aren't. There's no reason to have more than one template open at any one time."

Noonan hit the on/off switch and walked back over to the open files on the homing devices. "Are any homing devices missing?"

"You can see from the records there's only one missing and it was checked out the night of the robbery."

"But, were any others ones missing, maybe from weeks ago?"

"I see what you're digging for." Smith dug through the paperwork for a few minutes and then raised three fingers. "Three others. But records only go back five years."

"Is there any chance one of those wasn't really lost?"

"Of those three, no. Two of them came back destroyed and were dumped. The third was destroyed in a car bomb. I was on the car bomb case and I can assure you even if it wasn't destroyed in the explosion, it couldn't possibly have been operational."

"How long ago?"

"Three, four years ago. A while."

Noonan waved his hand at the paperwork. "So, according to these records, there is no way two homing devices could have been taken out of this office the night of the robbery."

"I'll count the devices myself." Smith wandered off and Noonan flicked his cellular phone open. Then he changed his mind. When Smith came back, Noonan was standing at the window watching the city trying to emerge from the fog.

"I physically counted the homing devices, Captain, er Heinz. There are four in use right now, one of them being our lost homing device. I called about the other three and they are in place and operational. None of them have anything to do with the bank robbery and all three have been in place for at least a week."

"I see." Noonan scratched his beard and then walked over to the map of San Francisco on the wall. "Smith, how many different facilities does the San Francisco Police have?"

"You mean like precincts and substations?"

"I mean like patrol car lots, repair facilities, impound yards, storage facilities."

"A dozen, maybe."

"Where are they?"

Smith ran through a laundry list of facilities, starting with patrol car storage and repair facility by the International Airport to the impound park near Lafayette Park. "Were you looking for anything in particular?"

"Tell me more about the storage facility in Hunter's Point. How large is it?"

"I don't really know. I've never been there. It's more for long-term storage than anything else. Did you want to go there?"

"Yes, right away."

Smith put the paperwork away and then joined Noonan as he walked out of the office. Once in the hallway but before they got to the downward stairs, Noonan put his hand on Smith's arm. "Wait here for a moment, please."

Smith stopped and then pointed further along down the hallway. "It's down there."

Noonan just smiled and went back to Property. He was gone for a moment and then came back to the stairwell.

"Did you forget something?" Smith asked.

Noonan shook his head. Halfway down the stairs Noonan stopped Smith. "Do you carry a gun?"

Smith pulled back her tweed jacket to reveal a .38 Special.

"Good."

"Do you think I'll need it? Should I call for backup?"

"No. Not yet. Just keep your eyes open."

Smith didn't say anything until they got into the car. As she pulled away from the parking lot and merged with the downtown traffic, she half turned to Noonan. "Captain, I don't want to add to your burdens but if there's going to be trouble, I'd like to be prepared. If there's going to be trouble, I'd suggest we have back-up."

Noonan was silent for a moment. "I'm not sure we need it."

"Well, the minute we do," Smith said. "I'd like you to tell me. No, make it that a minute before we need assistance. I don't like surprises, Captain, and this is the biggest case in years. We've ten lives on the line and up to $10 million missing."

Noonan was silent for a moment. "Well we can't go around causing a great commotion if there's nothing to report, can we? We're just going to take a look around the storage yard at Hunter's Point. If we see anything suspicious, we'll ask for back-up. Good enough?"

"Suits me. I'm just jumpy."

Smith was clearly not satisfied. Noonan could see a head shaking involuntarily out of the corner of his eye and a hand involuntarily reach for a sidearm and then move back to the wheel.

"But we've got to make one stop before we go to Hunter's Point."

Chapter 9

Strapping herself into the plastic chair which had more to do with safety than comfort, Greenleaf mumbled to herself as the truck went around some sharp turns. The other hostages clearly felt the same way because none of them had their hands in their laps. Everyone had a death grip on their seat belt.

"Death grip," Greenleaf muttered to herself. "How appropriate." It was gallows humor but it wasn't particularly funny.

Had the situation been different, perhaps if Greenleaf had been a Hollywood producer of comedies, the scene in the back of the truck would have been visually hilarious. The truck would drive straight and everyone would relax. This would only last until the vehicle slowed and then everyone would tense. Which way would the cab lurch? Would it be a sharp turn or a smooth sweep? Would the wheels find the curb? Would it slide on the wet cobblestones? Slower and slower the truck would go and each hostage would sink his and her fingers into a death grip on both ends of the seat belt strap which bound them to the wall of the cargo bay. Then the truck would make its turn and all ten hostages, five on either side of the hold, would lean in the direction of the turn. When the truck actually made the turn, the hostages on the inside of the turn would be pressed flat against their respective wall by centrifugal force.

On the other side, invisible hands would pull passengers forward until they were leaning well out over their own chairs. The truck would complete the turn and half the hostages would be settled gently back into the seats while the others would have to pull themselves back from hovering over the splintery floorboards. There would be a momentary respite of relief and then the process would begin again as the truck slowed for yet another turn.

Outside there was an ongoing cacophony of noise, most of it traffic. Vehicle engines whined by, horns honked and bus engines revved up. Once a trolley car clanged by. Occasionally all the hostages could hear was the drum of the truck's wheels on pavement. Once, when the truck came to a stop, they heard a snatch of a conversation, close enough to distinguish the voices were human but too distant to distinguish the words. Someone said they must be at a traffic light and suggested they bang on the side of the cargo hold. Before anyone had a chance to react, the truck lurched forward.

The dim light in the cargo interior cast an eerie gloom, which was accentuated by the guttural noises of fright from the hostages, male and female, young and old, macho and management. Not making circumstances any easier was the fact the van carried an odor, which was a cross between moldy lettuce and rabbit droppings tinged with just a hint of ammonia.

"It won't be long now," John's voice broke over the speaker in the cargo compartment. "You all know what to do. Just like last night, when I tell you to queue up, stand in a line at the back of the vehicle. The rear door will be unlocked and you are to walk straight forward. Do not look either way; just walk directly forward. Once again, make yourselves comfortable. You're going to be here for most of the day."

The truck made a few more lurches and then slowed, almost to walking speed. The going was smooth now and there was drumming coming from the wheels beneath the floor, like the truck was traveling over bricks. Gradually the vehicle slowed to a crawl and then stopped. But it was only for a second. Then it moved forward again at a crawl, the front of the truck rising as though it was stepping over a curb. A few seconds later the back wheels went up over the same bump. The sounds of the street were gone now, replaced by a rain of noise on the bottom of the truck.

"Must be gravel tossed up from the roadbed," said one of the vice presidents. No one else said anything. Vice presidents don't rate much of a response at banks, particularly Butterfield-Fargo where there were more vice presidents than lice on a punk rocker. Then there was some scraping on the side of the truck, as though the vehicle was going through a forest.

Finally the truck jerked to a stop. Gears ground and then the vehicle moved backward, slowly, until the rear tires felt some obstruction. The truck stopped and the light in the cargo hold went out.

"All right, ladies and gentlemen," came the voice from the darkness. "You know the drill so let's not have any problems. Line up. Wait for the tailgate to rise and walk forward. No wandering eyes, now."

Chapter 10

"I fingered the dials on the homing detector. "It's been a while since I've used one of these," She indicated a handful of homing devices, each about the size of a flashlight battery.

"How do we do that?" Noonan asked.

"Watch." Smith fiddled with the equipment while Noonan loitered about on the sidewalk in front of the electronics store. It was still a drizzly day but it appeared the sun was beginning to have its way with the fog bank. It certainly wasn't clearing in the sense Noonan could look up and see patches of blue sky, but the ground cover was growing wispy and its color was changing from nimbus and black to cumulus and white.

"Is it complicated?"

"Yes, when it has to be hexed, that is, set up. Once we lock in the code for the devices, it's just a matter of following the directional beam. Why did you buy a dozen homing devices? Wasn't one enough?"

"Maybe not," Noonan muttered.

Smith looked up from the homing equipment. "OK. I've identified all of the bugs with the same frequency. Now you understand if we use two of them at the same time we won't be able to tell which one is which."

"Not a problem."

"Now what?"

"Before we go, can you adjust this piece of machinery to be used as a bug detector, as if checking to see if there are any bugs in a room?"

"Y-y-y-e-e-s-s-s but it would be easier to use a detector specifically designed for the specific bug. We can buy one inside for about $300. Do you want one?"

77

Noonan shook his head. "Maybe not. Can you tell me if this is a bug?" Noonan handed Smith a small, round metal disk that looked like a camera battery.

"It looks like a camera battery."

"Ah, but is it?"

Smith played with some of the dials on the homing device detector. "I think it's a bug. Where did you get it?"

"Let's just say a friend gave it to me."

Ten minutes later, Smith pulled into traffic and began picking a route through the streets heading south. Crossing Market Street the dynamic duo in the unmarked car ducked under Highway 101 and headed south dodging the buses and trucks. The traffic was light but the streets were still slick. Noonan watched the traffic and settled into the comfort of the car seat. But it didn't last long. When they began the long run under Highway 101, he looked back.

"I know what you mean," Smith said. "I feel it too. I think it's the green Chevrolet. The one in front of the yellow cab."

"How long has it been there?"

"Don't know. I just started feeling like I was being watched. The Chev's been there ever since."

"I've always gone with my sixth sense, cut off to the right and let's do a wide circle. Then we'll see what happens. Just don't be too obvious about it."

Smith hit the right-hand turn signal and, at the next intersection, turned into the side street. Half a block later, the green Chevrolet followed. Noonan hummed a soft tune and waited for Smith to make the next turn, to the right again, and head back uptown. The Chevrolet made the same turn. But then again so did a yellow cab, a smoking Volkswagen and a motorcycle without a muffler eliciting a staccato of exhaust blasts.

"If he follows us through this next turn, he's definitely following us." Smith was watching the Chevrolet as it kept a safe distance behind them.

"What do you want me to do, call for back-up?"

"No. Not yet."

"OK, let's see what he does now." Smith signaled for another right turn and eased the car around the corner. Noonan watched a hand drifting to a pistol in a waistband.

"Don't shoot anyone yet, Detective."

Smith looked him sideways and smiled. As she did the green Chevrolet shot on by the corner. Though it was half a block back both Smith and

Noonan agreed they saw two figures in the front seat. Age, race, and sex were undetermined. If the two figures were looking at them, there was no way to tell. They just whipped by the corner and disappeared into the crush of yellow cabs, buses and a menagerie of clunkers none of which should have still been on the road.

"I almost thought we had something there," sighed Smith. "At least it would have been a lead."

"Don't be too sure it isn't. Let's pretend we were being followed. Take the long way to Hunter's Point. Weave around a bit. Do some double backing. Let's see if the Chevrolet shows up again."

Smith nodded and took the first left, drove two blocks and then pulled into a parking lot. The car was backed into a space which had a clear view of the street. Then the two waited patiently, watching the street.

"Tell me," Noonan said as he pulled gently on his beard. "Have you ever been to the storage yard?"

"A few times."

"Describe it to me."

"It's big and has all kinds of things all over the place, like bulldozers, burned out patrol cars, derelict vehicles. What do you want to know?"

"Are there any large structures?"

"Four or five warehouses. Large? I'd say they're about a ten feet long and 50 feet wide. Yeah. I guess you could call them large."

"I assume the whole area's fenced in. How about the approach to the storage area? Is it relatively open? Or do you have to drive down an alley to get to the front gate?"

"There's a long, sweeping approach but the last time I was there it was open, as in vacant lots on both sides of the road. I doubt it's been built up since then. After all, it is Hunter's Point."

"Meaning?"

"It's an inner city area, low income. An ethnic neighborhood."

"Ah," said Noonan sarcastically, "a black community where prosperity isn't just around the corner."

"Right."

"If you were going to intercept someone on the way into the storage yard, where would you do it?"

Smith gave Noonan a long look and said, "What do you know I should know?"

Noonan responded verbally. "Nothing I can tell you. It's just a hunch to be played out. If I'm correct, our friends in the green Chevrolet are going to be back. And they are not going to be very nice. Our lives may very well depend on just how well you remember the approach to the storage area."

"Why don't we just call for backup?"

"Because we can't get on the airwaves. The minute we get on the radio, those guys are gone. This may be our only chance to get a look at them."

"What makes you so sure anyone is going to take a shot at us? The green Chevy could have been some civilian on his way home."

"Could have been but I doubt it. And so do you. OK, let's take a chance. I think the hostages are being held in the storage area, probably in one of those warehouses you were talking about. I wasn't sure and then the green Chevy showed up. Now I'm certain."

"That's quite a stretch, Captain. If true, it also means someone in the Depart..."

"Correct, Detective. We've got some bad cops here. Think about it. Why is it one of the best police departments in the United States covering a city, which has water on three sides, can't find ten hostages? Every vehicle large enough to carry ten people has been stopped and searched for the past 48 hours and there hasn't been a clue. Why? The answer is obvious. What is the one vehicle large enough to carry ten hostages which wouldn't be searched?"

"A police vehicle!"

"Right. And what is the one place large enough to hold ten hostages the police wouldn't search?"

"A police storage yard." Smith snapped angrily. "It's so obvious now."

"Correct again. Let's suppose the hostages were taken out of the Greyhound bus at some location and put into a truck, maybe an old police transport vehicle. No one stops the truck because no one is thinking the hostages would be in a police vehicle. They drive to the police storage yard where the hostages are put in a converted warehouse. They only have to be held for a day or two so it doesn't matter who eventually finds out. It's like the person who's the inside man on the bank job. There are only three possibilities and two of them are hostages. When the hostages are released, the inside man is going to disappear. Ten hostages are taken, only nine are released. Nine, if the inside man is a hostage. Who cares if the police put two and two together next week? The man and money

Chapter 10

are gone. Figuring up to ten perps with $10 million tax-free – $1 million apiece. That's a lot of pina coladas."

"But if the hostages are at the storage yard and we get hit before we get in, we'll lose them. If we do call in, someone is going to pick it up on the radio. We're in a heck of a fix!"

"Ah, but not in the age of cyberspace," Noonan said sharply as he pulled his cellular phone from his pocket. "There is a way we can send a message without the perps knowing we are on to them."

"Very good. Just one question, though. How do you know I'm not with the bad guys?"

"It crossed my mind, Smith. Remember when I went back into the Property room after we left?"

"Yeah. When I thought you were looking for the men's room."

"I slipped back to see if anyone was getting on the phone. The property clerk was. If you were in with the bad guys, so to speak, you would have made a call."

"The call to the bad guys?"

"Right. One of the bad guys works in Property or used to work there."

"You mean the clerk?"

"Unlikely. She just wanted to let her superiors know a Captain Noonan from the Sandersonville Police Department was sniffing around the homing devices. Someone else put two and two together. If you were with them, there'd be no reason to tail us."

"I could still be one of the bad guys."

"No, Chief Thayer pulled you out of a lineup at random. So it's as good a chance as I've got at getting an honest cop. Right now the perp's job is to stop me before I get to the Hunter's Point Storage Yard. They know we're on the way there. By following us they were probably trying to figure a way to head us off before we were in the vicinity of the yard. They didn't want to make a hit near the storage yard because it would be like jumping up and down and yelling 'THE HOSTAGES ARE HERE!!' They wanted to do it somewhere else. They don't want to kill us, just stall us."

"How can you be so sure?"

"Smith, don't think like a cop. Think like a perp. These guys want to get out of town with the cash. They are going to keep those hostages until the last minute because they know we're going to put finding the hostages in front of finding the cash. The police aren't looking for the money; they're looking for hostages. After they've slipped the money out of town, those

81

hostages are going to be released. The perps are just playing for time. If we solve this in three days, fine. So what? It will be too late to catch them in town. Sooner or later the clues are going to give us the names of the perps and the inside men or women. But by then those people are going to be in Brazil or Tierra del Fuego."

"What does that have to do with not killing us if we get too close?"

"They can't kill us. In most cases, perps will be extradited if they have left the United States to avoid a murder charge. But if the perps are sitting in Rio de Janeiro and pumping millions into the local economy, well, the local police are going to have a very hard time finding them – at least until their money runs out. But if murders are involved, well, then the Rio police are going to have a whole other attitude."

"A lot of millions can buy a lot of lawyers."

"Right." Noonan smiled. "Sad but true."

"Fine. Now, clue me in. How did the perps know where we were going? If the clerk in Property isn't in on the caper then all she could have reported was you and I were looking at homing devices. No one even knew you were going back to the Police Department after the Greyhound Depot visit."

Noonan was silent for a moment. "You'll have to take it on trust. Let's just say I have every reason to believe I'm accurate."

Now it was Smith's turn to be silent. "Captain, I'm happy I'm not standing in your 12 1/2 Ds because the only thing I've seen is a green Chev which could have been following us."

"Faith, my child, faith. You've got to have faith." Noonan punched the Chief's number into the cellular phone. "But right now, get ready for the ride of your life!"

Chapter 11

The High Lord of English Petroleum Robert Harrah stood at his window, looking down on San Francisco when his secretary buzzed him. At English Petroleum, secretaries were still called secretaries. The only sign the company had moved into the 90s was they were called Ms. Smith and Ms. Jones rather than Harriet and Charlene. But the pay was still the same.

"I have Billingsley on the ground floor, Mr. Harrah. He is alone. Shall I send the elevator for him?"

Harrah didn't bother to turn around. "Absolutely, Ms. Chesney. Hold my calls until we're through."

"Yes, sir."

Harrah turned toward his desk and strode to the far side of the teak island. He pulled a cigar out of a sandalwood humidor on the shelf behind his desk. It was a Churchillian in size but Cuban in content. He nipped the end of the tube with a cigar knife and dropped the plug into a small waste basket on the floor immediately beneath the humidor. Striking a wood match on the underside of his desk he let the sulfur burn away before running the flame back and forth beneath the cigar. Then he lit the cigar with deep, slow breaths. When the tag end of the leaves glowed with embers, he shook the match out.

The silence of the room was broken only by the hum of the upcoming elevator. By the time Billingsley was in the office, Harrah was already on his black leather throne, a potentate of paper, and on his desk spread in suits like tarot cards, were the fates and fortunes of his empire. His cigar lay at an angle in the Kobuk jade ashtray sending a single column of smoke straight to the ceiling.

The elevator disgorged Billingsley with a pop. He nodded at Harrah for a moment then hunched his cadaverous frame across the dark carpet to one of the leather chairs opposite Harrah. There were no pleasantries because none were needed.

"Hopkins has been busy."

"I kind of expected that." Harrah sucked on his cigar and leaned back in his chair as far as it would go. "Americans are so predictable." He shook his head arrogantly. "Police force for the world but they can't pull off a simple bank heist."

Billingsley chuckled. "Maybe they're all from Wigan. What do you expect for a nation spending more time with Reader's Digest and the National Enquirer than an evening newspaper?" He looked over his shoulder, across the room and out the window at fog-shrouded San Francisco. "At least it's clear up here."

Harrah smiled and indicated with a wave of his hand full of cigar that Billingsley was to begin his report.

"Hopkins left here, bee-lined to a police storage lot in Hunter's Point. Actually it is more like a salvage yard. In America they call it a junkyard."

"How appropriate."

"Yes, sir. There were about thirty vehicles in the enclosure, most of them police vehicles, which had clearly been there for a while. Many of them had flat tires. Others were jammed into open carports and were covered with dust. There were three large warehouses, each 10,000 to 15,000 square feet, which were enclosed."

"Large enough to hold hostages?"

"Yes. In fact they probably did."

"This is beginning to fit like a ball of wax. Go on."

"Hopkins pulled up to the front gate, rang a bell and talked a man who came out of one of the large warehouses. The man went back inside and came out with two other men, one of them in a police uniform. There was a very brief conversation at the gate and then all four men went to a coffee shop on Market Street. Then..."

"Market Street? That's halfway across town. Why didn't they find a local pub?"

"Hunter's Point is thick with wogs."

"Hardly a place for white faces, eh?"

Chapter 11

"Or flatties. The discussion in the coffee shop was short, less than time for a cup of coffee. Almost in and out – like a bad marriage. Then all four came out of the coffee shop and carried the conversation out to the sidewalk. It was loud enough for me to catch snatches of it across the street. They were hot. It got so bad the man in the police uniform looked up and down the sidewalk and then dashed away. Then there were three men left on the sidewalk. At this point they were almost yelling. Hopkins and the two other men were so animated people were walking around them on the sidewalk."

"Certainly hit a nerve with the sharper, didn't we?"

"Did indeed. Whatever they were talking about came to a bloody halt when one of the two men with Hopkins got a call on his cell phone. Whatever it was, it was more important than what I presume to be the ten million dollars because Hopkins and one of the men with whom he was talking just broke away and sprinted to the car where the man in the police uniform was sitting. They talked for a second and then Hopkins left and walked casually back to his car. The other man jumped into the car with the man in the police uniform, a green Chevy, and they drove away. The last guy just stood there on the sidewalk in front of the coffee shop."

"There were two cars? I thought Hopkins took the men in his car."

"Nope. Separate cars. I ran the plates on both. Hopkins car is registered to Hopkins." Billingsley pulled a small, leather notebook out of his jacket pocket and flicked it open professionally. "The green Chevy has plates registered to the Salamander Pet Salon in the Sunset District. But the plates are for a minivan."

"A pet shop? Minivan?"

"Hardesty ran a check on it. The pet shop was burned out of business about six months ago. Suspicious circumstances. I'm assuming the plates came from an impounded vehicle."

"How did you run the check on the plates so fast?"

"Hardesty hooked his laptop to his cellular phone. Did it while he was watching the green Chevrolet. Technology has come up quite a notch since the days of the ten-cent phone call. It's all a matter of being able to log into the right networks. Our security clearance here gets us onto the Police Department's crime computer."

"Clever boy. Did you decide to follow Hopkins or the two men in the green Chevrolet?"

"Both. Hardesty took the car and followed Hopkins. I took my chances with a yellow cab."

"Wasn't it a bit risky?"

"Following a policeman in a car with false plates? I didn't think so. Hopkins was our quarry so someone had to follow him. The others were icing on the cake. Anything we learned from them would be valuable. Besides, when I get a chance to take a peek at the other man's cards, I do it."

Harrah smiled for a split second and then he frowned. "Hopkins is playing us for fools. Or at least he thinks he is. I don't like his attitude. It makes me very nervous when I have to deal with a stupid man. He's not smart enough to know everyone pays for anyone's mistake." He took a deep drag on his cigar. "Where did Hopkins go?"

"The San Francisco Police Department. He parked his Mercedes 210 and disappeared inside. He stayed inside for about 20 minutes and then all heck broke loose. Hardesty called me later and said he didn't hear anything on the radio scanner so he had to assume there had been some kind of a call on a cellular phone. Hopkins came out with the police Chief and a dozen officers. They hit the streets and went Code 3 – sirens and lights – all the way back to same Hunter's Point salvage yard where we had been earlier in the day."

"What happened there?"

"I don't know. The last I heard from Hardesty was half an hour ago. He was still near the salvage yard. He could see a lot of activity but did not know what was happening. Or at least he couldn't see what was happening."

"Hopkins?"

"Hardesty says his car is still at the salvage yard." Billingsley looked at his watch. "At least he was 15 minutes ago. There's only one exit and he hadn't seen anyone come out yet so he assumed Hopkins was still inside. The fact I haven't heard from Hardesty means nothing has happened."

"The money?"

"I can speculate and it's too early to be rash."

"Granted. Anything else?"

"My trip was strange and I don't know what to make of it. Once again, I can only speculate."

"Go ahead, I am just dying for a good mystery." Harrah took another drag on his cigar and blew a giant, whirling smoke ring.

"As soon as the second man, the one without the police uniform got into the green Chevrolet and pulled away, the man in the police uniform

Chapter 11

got into the back seat. I didn't see him for about three or four minutes but I could see he was doing something in the back seat. When he crawled back into the front seat, he wasn't wearing a police uniform anymore."

"He changed in the back seat?"

"Yes."

"Did your cabbie notice?"

"He was too busy talking about how he'd always wanted to drive someone who said follow that car!"

"Probably thought it was a Hollywood thriller."

"Actually he did say something similar. Then he said, 'where's the camera crew?'"

"But he didn't see the man change clothes?"

"If he did he didn't mention it to me when he talked with me later. I didn't either, actually. The only reason I know he changed clothing was because I had seen him in a uniform up close. At 30 or 40 yards, he could have been doing anything in the back seat."

"Where did they go?"

"Nowhere right away. They knew where they were going because for the first five minutes they went straight, with determination. They were speeding until they got under Highway 101, then they slowed to a crawl. And I mean a crawl. We were going so slow cars were honking at them and us. Cabbie explanation it was great, inching along, running up more on the clock than on the rue. Then the two men spotted an unmarked police car and started following it, matching its speed about a block back."

"How do you know it was an unmarked car?"

"City plates. Could have been sewer and water or telephone but I guessed it was police. If Hardesty had been with me I would have run the plates."

"Go on."

"We followed the car for about three miles and suddenly the police car picked up speed, took a couple of wild turns like they'd made the tail."

"Do you think they had?"

"They acted like they did."

"Who was in the other car?"

"I'll get to the other car in a little bit. Let me finish this line of thought first." Billingsley looked at Harrah for permission not to answer the question right away. Harrah nodded his consent. Billingsley continued, "As soon as it looked like the green Chevrolet had been made, the car just drove on by when the pigeon made the last turn."

"Did you see who was inside the pigeon, as you call him?"
"There were two of them but no, I didn't see who they were."
"You saw them later?"
"About 20 minutes later, I'm just getting to that."
"Tell me about the people in the unmarked car now."
"Two of them. One, the driver, was a wog like a mud fence. About 35, not tall, not small, hard to tell in a moving car. The other was a white guy, maybe 60, salt-and-pepper beard, tall but not fat, black leather jacket."
"Captain Noonan of the Sandersonville Police Department. He's the law and order guru" which Harrah pronounced gar-eu – "called in by Police Chief Thayer. He was in here asking for our assistance." "Oh, how rich." Billingsley laughed.
"Nothing happened to him, I hope? He's our secret weapon. If Hopkins can't get the money, Noonan will."
"Well, he's in very great danger. After the men in the green Chevrolet let the pigeon fly, they drove back toward the salvage yard in Hunter's Point. But they didn't drive into the yard. They pulled into a dark alley about two blocks in front of the entrance to the salvage yard. It was dark in the alley so I could barely see the car. Clearly their intention. They waited for about 15 minutes and then suddenly it blasted out. I couldn't see what happened until the very last second. They were aiming to sideswipe a car. As it turned out, the car was the pigeon with the wog and Noonan. The Chevrolet smacked the unmarked car hard. Probably would have killed one of them if the driver hadn't been fast.

It was almost like they were expecting the accident." "How bad was it?" Harrah was suddenly concerned.

"It was certainly smash and dash. It looked bad from where I was. One instant the Chevrolet was hiding out in the alley and the next it was slamming into the unmarked police car. Then, in the next instant the green Chevrolet was off and away, roaring through the streets of Hunter's Point. The unmarked car tried to follow but lost the Chevrolet pretty quickly. So I hooked onto the unmarked car. As I was following it, I ran into a swarm of police cars, Code 3, moving in the opposite direction toward the salvage yard. Hopkins passed me going toward the salvage yard. The unmarked car went directly to San Francisco General Hospital. The two passengers went inside. Then I came here."

Chapter 12

Candice Greenleaf was not a happy camper when she opened her eyes and saw her new abode. Further, to say she was displeased would have been a gross understatement. Appalled would have been more appropriate. While the dormitory where they had spent the night was, at the very least, a civilized setting, this domicile was clearly designed only for sitting.

"This looks like an abandoned butcher shop." Cheri Molk ran her fingers along the dust-covered glass and peered through the cupboards into the open, dry, warm freezers. "How long do you think this place has been abandoned?"

"I don't want to think about how long it's been abandoned," someone said sarcastically behind her. "I only want to know how long it will be before we can abandon it."

"Not soon enough," snapped Greenleaf. "Let's have a look around."

For the next two minutes the ten hostages picked their way around the display cases, freezers, generators and hanging wires. It was as long as it took them to discover all of the doors were locked and there were no windows to test. There was no electricity and the sole source of illumination came from a large skylight 25 feet off the floor. The only amenities for the hostages were ten metal folding chairs set against a wall, a large grocery bag full of toilet paper and paper towels in the bathroom, and a pile of newspapers and magazines.

Greenleaf picked up one of the newspapers and looked at its date. "At least they got us today's paper." She held the newspaper up so the branch president could see the headline, VANISHING GREYHOUND

FOUND, HOSTAGES STILL MISSING. "It's certainly nice to know someone knows we're still missing."

"This is one heck of a place to keep hostages," one of the tellers said to no one in particular.

"Maybe," replied Greenleaf. "What it looks like is a Plan B holding facility. Someplace to hold us if we had to be moved. Clearly something is happening out there."

"Well, maybe it could happen a little faster," Molk said as she unfolded a metal chair and sat down heavily. "I've got a date this evening I'd hate to miss. What day is today anyway?"

Chapter 13

It took Chief Thayer until noon to catch up with Captain Noonan. The raid on the Hunter's Point Storage Yard had eaten up most of the morning and then dealing with the press and the FBI took what was left. As far as the hospital was concerned, there was nothing he could do about Noonan or Smith's condition. He didn't even know what conditions those were; he just knew they had reported into the hospital. Noonan had told him as much on the police band. For the moment he didn't have time to find out. If they were at the hospital they were being treated and that was the most he could expect.

The raid on the storage yard had raised as many questions as it had settled. A quick check of the buildings revealed one converted into living quarters for at least ten people. Ten cots were found, which led to this obvious conclusion the hostages had been sequestered there. But the room was clean of any indication it had been used recently. There was no garbage. All the chairs were stacked in a corner and the card tables were folded and slipped behind the chairs. Each of the cots had a blanket neatly folded on its futon. The mirrors and toilets were clean. The only suspicious aspect of the room was a clean floor. Dust indeed would have settled if the room had been left vacant for any extended period of time.

Then one of the patrolmen found a Butterfield-Fargo First deposit slip. This sent the lab team into the room. The murky picture was muddied further when an APB located the damaged green Chevrolet in the crowded parking lot of the San Francisco General Hospital. The plates were traced to a defunct pet store in the Sunset District. But the plates were for a minivan so the alert patrolman had fed the vehicle registration number into the crime computer. There was a match. The Chevrolet was traced to a wrecking yard in Oakland where records indicated it had been destroyed the previous year.

Still missing were the perps, $10 million in cash, the contents of the safety deposit boxes and the hostages.

But the clues were mounting.

The Chief hitched a ride with Hopkins and they made it to San Francisco General Hospital without incident although it appeared Hopkins was working very hard on taking as much advantage as he could out of having the police Chief on board. To Hopkins' evident dismay, they were not flagged to the curb once because they didn't see a cop all the way from the Hunter's Point Salvage Yard to San Francisco General.

"Can't find one when you need one."

"What's that?" the Chief asked as Hopkins whipped through town, sliding over the trolley tracks.

"Cops, Chief. I always wanted a Code 3 escort and I figured today would be as close as I'll ever get."

"If you keep driving this way we'll be getting a police escort to the morgue. What's the hurry?"

"I've still got $10 million reasons to worry about what's going to happen next."

"It's only a business loss, Douglas. No sense in getting riled up over money."

"It's not just money," Hopkins said in a normal tone. "It's **Money!!** A $10 million loss plus the safety deposit losses are not going to look good on my resume."

"Well, the good news is Captain Heinz Noonan is on the job. In the past 24 hours he's done all right."

"Yeah, but where's the money?"

"I don't know. But I'll bet he does. You can ask him at the hospital."

But Noonan wasn't at the hospital.

Neither was Detective Smith. Smith's unmarked police car was in the parking lot, badly smashed, but neither Smith nor Noonan were in the hospital. Neither had been checked in nor been examined. Chief Thayer pulled his cellular out of his pocket and punched in Noonan's number.

"I was wondering when you were going to call," Noonan's voice answered the phone without a salutation. "Where are you?"

Chapter 13

"Undercover. Actually I'm having lunch with Detective Smith on Fisherman's Wharf."

"You're supposed to be in the hospital!"

"The hospital is for sick people. I'm doing just fine." Noonan chortled a bit.

"Any news of the hostages? "The Chief was hopeful.

"Not yet," Noonan replied. "But we do need to meet."

"Tell me where you are and I'll join you."

"Are you alone?"

"I can be." The Chief looked over his shoulder at Hopkins who was trying to charm the admitting nurse who was going over the logbooks name-by-name for the past six hours.

"Be sure you come alone." Noonan then gave him the name of the restaurant.

"That restaurant is not on Fisherman's Wharf."

"Neither am I. Smith and I are on the move. Keep the name of the restaurant to yourself. There are too many leaks in this case as it is."

"OK. Good lead on the Hunter's Point Salvage..." But his compliment came too late. Noonan had snapped off his cellular.

Losing Hopkins was easy. The Chief said he was going and Hopkins waved good-bye, barely looking up from the admissions book.

Noonan and Smith were sitting in the back of the Wharf-and-Compass when the Chief came in. This particular restaurant was not one the Chief would have chosen for any kind of a meeting, clandestine or otherwise. Half of the restaurant was dedicated to college-age beer drinkers and the rest was designed for the just-above-college-age white wine cooler drinkers. All of it was dark enough to be mistaken for a coal mine.

Chief Thayer made it into Wharf-and-Compass and stood for a long moment near the front door waiting for his eyes to adjust to the darkness. Then he skirted the main part of the room looking at the tables pressed up against the walls. He found Noonan and Smith in one of the corner booths. As soon as Chief Thayer showed up, Smith got up and went to the counter.

"Smith isn't joining us for lunch?"

"Not just yet," replied Noonan. "We've got some critical matters to discuss."

"Really?" The Chief voiced surprise.

The Matter of the Vanishing Greyhound

"Now, George. Time is short so let's have a little bit of honesty here. Why am I really on this case?"

"I needed your help. You're the best person..."

Noonan shook his head sadly. "No. George. Let me tell you why I'm here. I'm here because I work alone and you know someone highly placed in your Department" – and Noonan stressed the words highly placed – "is involved. Most of what I am doing any of your men – or women – could do. Yeah, the vanishing bus was a bit out of your line, but basically, it's not unsolvable given enough time. But the robbery is not why I'm here, is it?"

"It has crossed my mind I might have an inside leak."

"No, George. It didn't just cross your mind. You don't have an inside leak. You have an inside tidal wave. That's why you like the idea of cell phones. I call you and that's as far as the conversation goes. If you're as good as your reputation, you've been watching some people carefully."

"OK. You're right. I am watching one particular person carefully. But right now I don't have..."

"Yeah, I know. Right now, George, you've got to solve a crime the newspapers are calling the 'Crime of the Century.'"

Noonan picked up a newspaper and plopped it down on the table between them. "So far you've come up empty-handed. The perps are still missing in spite of the fact there's been a two-day dragnet. The hostages are still the entire Most Wanted List, $10 million in cash is still missing, the contents of the safety deposit boxes are still running around San Francisco – maybe – and no one has come up with an explanation as to how a Greyhound bus can drive onto the Golden Gate Bridge with police cars in hot pursuit and then disappear into thin air. This, George, is not one of your finest moments."

"You're right. The main reason I asked you to come to San Francisco."

"A good idea. But having me here is not going to do you any good unless you clean up your Department. Bad cops have got to go. One bad apple will spoil the entire barrel."

"I can't clean anything out without proof." Chief Thayer shook his head. "I can't just shut someone down because of what I know, particularly at the level we're talking about here. I've got to have proof."

"Carefully done, you'll get the proof you need. But we are still a long way from making an arrest. If this were a normal crime, a simple one, we'd have no problem at all. We could walk right in, make arrests and allow the natural course of events to occur. But if we did, we'd only get one or two

Chapter 13

of the perps and without the English Petroleum $10 million, the hostages, or the contents of the safety deposit boxes."

"Do you know who the perps are?"

"If you mean by name, no. But the fog is clearing. I'd say there are at least eight. There were the four who took down the bank and at least one someone in the Police Department, probably working in Property, associated with Property or has worked in Property. The someone in the police department had to have access to the homing devices and the tracking apparatus. I can't prove anything because the homing device put on the Greyhound is gone. There might have even been two tracking devices, one given to the perps and the other put on the bus. But the one put on the bus was disabled. Then there's the inside man at the bank. Then there is someone highly placed who is calling the shots. But you already know you've got a bad apple."

"I figured the same. What about the inside man at the bank?"

"There isn't one. Most likely it's Hopkins. He had access to all the information concerning the bank and its security arrangements. The critical information was included in the paperwork I read last night – hidden but there. English Petroleum confirmed it as well. Hopkins had access to the security tapes and it would not have been hard for him to switch them on Saturday – or even Monday. He could go where he wanted with no one the wiser. After all, he's the insurance man. If we ever find the tape I'm betting it's not going to show anything at all."

"What?"

"See, George, what bothered me from the first wasn't that I didn't have enough clues. I had too many. Finally I figured it out. What we have here is a triple robbery. First, whatever English Petroleum is pulling is illegal. Sure the IRS knows they have lots of money in cash sitting around, but I'll bet the IRS doesn't know why. Right now I'd say ol' pompous ass Harrah is sweating square nails. He's got paperwork on $10 million in cash which shows incorrect serial numbers."

"What makes you think so? "The Chief thought about it. "Even if it's true, so what?"

"Look at it logically. Whatever English Petroleum is doing involves lots and lots of cash. So they get the cash from a bank – or the federal government. But it's inconvenient for a bank to give them $10 million in unmarked bills. The easiest thing for the banks to do is just order $10 million from the U.S. Mint. The feds are happy because they have the serial numbers so they can trace any illegal activity. English Petroleum can't ask for unmarked bills without raising suspicions. So they take the marked bills and slowly launder them, replacing the known serial numbers with untraceable serial numbers."

"Why would they do that?"

Noonan was about to respond when a waiter finally made it over to their table. "What took you so long," Chief Thayer asked. "Did you get lost in the dark?"

"Very funny." The waiter looked at the two men and then glanced at Smith sitting at the bar. "Aren't you three a bit old for this kind of an establishment?"

"Nope," replied Noonan. "But you don't stay employed asking snippy questions of your customers. And this is a bad day to be annoying the two of us."

"Oh, I am so frightened," the waiter said. "Frighten me some more and I'll call the cops."

"No need," said Chief Thayer reaching for his badge. "I am the cops. Now, why don't you be a good little boy and get us two luncheon specials or I'm going to make the owner of this establishment a very unhappy camper."

The badge stalled the waiter. He stood for a moment in the darkness unable to think of anything to say. The Chief waited, his badge still dangling in his hand. The long, pregnant pause was only broken when Noonan started laughing. "You can go now. You've shown us how polite you are."

The waiter was still about to say something then changed his mind. He just backed away into the darkness.

"I wonder what he's going to do to our luncheon special?" Chief Thayer asked hesitantly.

"Don't worry about it, George. If you don't like it you can shoot him."

Chief Thayer laughed. "You have always been a card, Heinz. I'd like to spend more leisure time with you, but, heck, I'm up to my ears in banana peels right now. Let's go back to English Petroleum. Why should they care about what serial numbers are on the bills?"

"Because they don't want any of the cash traced back to them, especially from overseas. Take the $100 bill with the serial number 12345, for example. On paper the U.S. Mint has given it to English Petroleum. English Petroleum figures out some way to exchange 12345 for 6789, like laundering it through a bank. 12345 goes into circulation in the United States and disappears into the economy while 6789 goes to pay off a foreign dignitary to ease a contract. The feds will never see 12345 coming in from a foreign country because it's already been switched with 6789. Thus there will be no way to trace the actual dollars which were given to English Petroleum by the U.S. Mint."

"It's a bit far-fetched, Heinz. Why wouldn't English Petroleum just write a check and let the dignitaries cash the check in some American bank – or an English bank or any other kind of a bank?"

"Because they're not dealing with honorable people. They're probably dealing with corrupt officials who have to pass along part of the booty to drug smugglers, murderers, blackmailers and lawyers. These guys have to wash whatever money they get so they can't be seen walking into a bank with a check for $10 million. The primary reason they need the cash is so it can be quickly and easily broken into smaller, usable amounts."

Chief Thayer scratched his head. "So with the bank hit and the $10 million gone, English Petroleum runs the risk of having its entire scheme exposed to the worst of all people, the IRS."

"Right! Once the insurance company pays off, the IRS will be on the lookout for bill number 12345. When it and lots and lots of its buddies show up in the United States, the IRS is going to start wondering how so many bills could be showing up in so many different areas. Worse yet, all they have to do is account for one bill that was in someone's possession before the date of the robbery. Then English Petroleum will be in a world of hurt."

The Chief smiled. "I see what you mean. English Petroleum now has a major problem. If the money is found and the serial numbers do not match the invoice, they're guilty of laundering money. If the money is not found and the insurance company pays off, sooner or later those original bills are going to find their way into circulation. Once again, it's bad news for English Petroleum."

"Right. They're between a rock and a hard place. They can't get the original bills back because they are long gone. But they have to get the bogus bills back to prove to the IRS everything is hunky dory. Getting a check for the loss isn't going to do them any good; they need proof the money stolen was returned."

"But the only way they're going to get the money back with no questions asked is to cut a deal with the perps." The Chief scratched his head and nodded.

"That, George, is the rub. If they can find them, yes." Noonan looked up as the waiter brought their lunch. The waiter clearly wasn't happy and he didn't say anything when he dropped two plates covered with the identical fare in front of the men. He didn't bother to wait to see if either man wanted something to drink.

"Shoot him, George," Noonan said. "It will kill me to eat Brussels sprouts."

"If you wanted meat you should have gone to a steak house."

"Actually I wanted barbecued salmon on the banks of the Kenai River but here I am in the city by the bay." Noonan smiled as he spoke.

Chief Thayer picked through his lunch with his fork and then put it aside. "You're right, Heinz. I should shoot him."

Both men laughed as they pushed their plates aside. Chief Thayer leaned forward. "Heinz, the easiest way to wash money would be through someone who had access to a bank but didn't actually work there. Someone like Hopkins."

"You catch on quickly. Now, follow this. Hopkins knows about the laundering scheme because he's doing it. I mean, he probably got the English Petroleum account because he would do it. He gets a nice fat account and all he has to do is something legal. He exchanges legal $100 bills. So he develops avenues with people who can launder the money. They're more than happy to do it because he's paying a percentage and they're not doing anything illegal."

Noonan took a breath and then took another look at his lunch. Thayer took a look at his special and both men looked up at each other – and then they laughed. Noonan continued, "Hopkins had money to burn so he used the connections he had to generate other clients. Which in turn generated other clients, some of them unsavory. In the process of handling all this money, he makes the critical connection, to the perps. More likely the perps approached him. All he has to do was play along and he'd walk away with a million bucks. No one gets hurt, except his company of course, but why should Hopkins care? I'll bet he thought the robbery would happen, no one would suspect him, and he'd end up with the million in cash and still have English Petroleum as a client."

"Pretty gutsy move for him, Heinz. I can see the rest of this coming. One of the perps gets in touch with my man in Property. Everybody gets greedy and a simple $10 million snatch turns into a full-fledged robbery complete with hostages and a razzle-dazzle escape."

Chapter 13

"Exactly," Noonan said as he wadded a paper napkin in his hand. "Hopkins doesn't know the inside man in the Police Department. There's no reason he had to know. Why the razzle-dazzle escape, as you call it? Because the robbery is a pretty basic grab and dash. What the perps need is confusion in the Police Department and time. They got the confusion with the disappearance of the Greyhound on the Golden Gate Bridge and they got the time because your priority is to find those hostages, not look for the money. Where did they put the hostages? The one place the police would not search."

"In a police storage yard."

"Right. I'll bet the green Chevrolet and the truck used to transport the hostages have been there as well."

"But how did they know we were about to close in on the hostages? I didn't order the raid until I got the call from you."

"One of my little secrets. I'll tell you about it later."

"OK." The Chief thought for a moment. "But all this still doesn't tell us why there are hostages. The perps have the money. Why do they need the hostages?"

"I'm not sure but there are two possibilities. One, the perps don't know where the money actually is. Hopkins is no fool. If the perps have the money they could disappear and leave him with nothing but a jail sentence. Hopkins could have the money in a safe location. The perps don't know where it is. The second possibility – and the more likely scenario I believe – is the perps are going to sell back the stolen money to English Petroleum. It makes more sense. They're holding the hostages to give themselves time to make the exchange and give Hopkins and the inside people at the Police Department time to get away clean. There's some kind of timetable in play. We just don't know what it is."

"Sounds logical," the Chief said as he nodded. "Where do we go from here?"

"We follow the money, of course. The three key characters are Hopkins, the suspect in the property office, and whoever at English Petroleum is going to make the connection to the perps." Noonan broke down and took a taste of his lunch. Chief Thayer just watched. When Noonan put his fork down the Chief smiled.

"You do want me to shoot the waiter, right?"

It was Noonan's turn to smile. "Yeah, and make it dum dum."

The Chief scratched his head. "Among a lot of things, Heinz. I can see the three crimes you are talking about but I don't see the connections."

"There are none, George. They just occurred. At first I thought I was investigating a robbery but there were just too many loose ends for only one. Then I realized I was looking at more than one. Then things began to make sense."

"Well, I agree with you there are a lot of loose ends. But how does what English Petroleum is doing overseas have to do with a Greyhound bus vanishing on the Golden Gate Bridge?"

"Nothing. That's what makes this case so intriguing. Nothing seems to fit unless you consider there are three crimes. For instance, why is English Petroleum so uncooperative? Any other company would be providing all the help we needed to locate and identify their money. The faster their money is identified, the faster they get it back—or the insurance pays off. But English Petroleum is acting like they don't care if they ever see the $10 million again. Why? One of two reasons. First, they really do not want to see the money again, which I don't believe or, second, they are expecting to make contact with the perps."

"Or the perps are from English Petroleum in the first place."

"Not likely. For the robberies to make sense, there are only two inside people, Hopkins and the cop from Property. They don't need any more than the two cops and every extra person means one more split and greater risk. Hopkins is in the key position. He can talk to both the perps and English Petroleum. But he's not a cop."

"You're putting a lot of faith in Hopkins being the inside man."

"Yes I am. But I don't have much of a choice. What have you got on your man in the Department? Enough to send him away?"

"In a word: no. There's a difference between what I know and what I can prove. Until he makes some kind of a stupid move, I'll have to be content with forcing him out – with a full pension."

"Then Hopkins is our key. But we have to be careful because he is playing a very dangerous game. He's going to have to negotiate with two groups of people who have very little appreciation for the other. The perps have a time table. They have to get out of town. No matter how careful they have been, there are enough clues for the cops to find them eventually. It's just going to take some time. I'm betting English Petroleum has already been contacted about their dollars. I'm sure they're going to be offered some kind of a quiet deal. English Petroleum gets its money back and the perps get a percentage kickback. Everyone's happy except Capital Assurance and Fidelity, Inc."

"A lot of speculation, Heinz, but I don't have a better idea. But you are right about one thing. The only apparent solid lead we've got is Hopkins. We can find him and we can follow him."

"Sooner or later he's going to lead us to the money." Noonan nodded his head slowly.

"But I need those hostages before I need the money."

"Believe me, George. When we find the money we'll find the hostages. That's their bargaining chip. Those hostages won't be released until the last possible minute – and in a manner designed to confuse us."

"So you follow Hopkins. Plan A?"

"Uh, huh. We've rented a couple of cars for that purpose. You might say we're going to play their game back at them."

Noonan stood up and waved at Detective Smith. As Smith came over and sat down Noonan pulled two sets of keys from his jacket pocket. "Two cars, George, both rented in Smith's name, so there's no way anyone can trace the plates very quickly."

"Somehow I don't feel you two are telling me everything." The Chief looked at the keys and wrote down the license numbers. "A purple Subaru? Give me a break, Smith. Don't you think a purple Subaru a bit conspicuous?"

"You could say so." Noonan gave a mischievous smile.

The Chief looked from Smith to Noonan. "OK. You two do what you have to. But I want to know the minute you have anything solid. Those hostages are still our first concern. I don't want any screw-ups. And keep using the cellular phones. I don't trust the police radio yet."

"Fine, Chief. We'll let you know the minute anything happens. But, there is just one more thing I need you to do."

"Shoot."

Noonan reached beside him and lifted his leather jacket off the chair next to him. "I seem to have lost a button from my jacket. Could you see it's replaced and the jacket sent back to my room at the St. Francis?"

The Chief looked at Noonan with an incredulous stare. "You want me to have your jacket button replaced? At a time like this?"

"Correct. And then have the jacket sent back to my room at the St. Francis Hotel."

"Well, yes, I suppose I could do that." The Chief looked from the leather jacket to Noonan to Smith and then back to the jacket. "There's a tailor I know in Chinatown who can do it right away."

"Excellent. And have it sent back to my room at the St. Francis Hotel the moment it's finished, right? As soon as the button is replaced. Back to the St. Francis Hotel. Right away. Even if it has to go by cab."

"Sure, Heinz. I am supposed to pick something up from this request?"

"No. I just need the button on before I fly out this evening. You can have it done, can't you?" Noonan looked as Smith gave a nod of his head toward the door.

"Sure."

The Chief continued to give Noonan an incredulous look as Detective Smith looked at the lunch of the two men sitting on the table. "You guys didn't finish your lunch."

Noonan and Chief Thayer looked sideways at each other and then at Smith. "Yes and no," replied Noonan. "Actually we didn't even start."

Noonan rose quickly and made sure Chief Thayer had his jacket. "It's very important, let me emphasize, I have the button on this jacket repaired before I go this evening. You can take care of it, can't you George?"

Then Noonan left George Thayer, Chief of the San Francisco Police, one of the largest, most sophisticated police departments in America, seated at a vegetarian bar with a leather jacket missing a button folded over his arm and a look of incredulity on his face.

Chapter 14

Even though it was early afternoon, fog still shrouded the streets of San Francisco. But the fog only hovered at street level. Forty floors up, the sun began to peek through the wispy top of the layer of fog and sixty floors up, it was as if there was no city, simply an ocean of churning gray froth washing the horizon with nothing save the spires of skyscrapers which rose like teeth from the mouth of a dragon. Far to the north where its uprights were hidden by the angle of view, the rise and fall of the cables of the Golden Gate Bridge appeared as a pair of giant snakes swimming in tandem in the sea of gray mist. At 123 floors up, Harrah was standing at his office window looking down on the city like a lord surveying his fief. At his elevation, the sun hung like a giant, sphere of fire, its heat blasting through his office window like sunlight through a magnifying glass. Though the window was cold to the touch, inside his office it was so hot the air conditioner was set at ten. With his arms outstretched as though he was about to fly, Harrah, dressed in a jet black silk suit, appeared as a cutout against the blistering sunshine to Billingsley and Hardesty who sat in matching leather chairs before the president's desk.

"This is not a good day." Harrah placed his hands into the pockets of jacket with elegance, as if he had a raw egg in each hand. Leaving the window, he glided rather than walked across the Persian carpets and settled behind the teak desk. "But nothing less than could have been expected."

"Did the perp say where the exchange was to take place?" Hardesty leaned his butterball torso back against the leather chair.

"No. They just asked if we were interested in an exchange, our original $10 million for $5 million in smaller bills."

"Clever." Billingsley smiled. "We give them five. They give us ten. We collect another 10 in insurance. It keeps us from being very cooperative with the authorities and it gives them a clear $5 million."

"Too clever. Too clever. Clearly they know we have to get the specific bills of the $10 million back. It means we have to deal with them. Play the game their way."

"The flip side is also true, sir. If they don't deal with us, we'll hunt them down and we don't have to know who Ernesto A. Miranda was."

"It doesn't mean we won't. It just means we won't have the incentive."

"We can trust them, right?" Hardesty ran his finger nails along the crease in his sharkskin suit, which ran over the bulge in his midsection. He looked as though he had a bowling ball concealed under his jacket.

Billingsley snickered.

Harrah leaned back in his chair. "Oh, I trust them," he said. "It's whether they can trust us."

"No honor among thieves, eh?" Billingsley leaned forward and began tapping his bony fingers on the desk. "No matter how we do this it's going to be tricky. I don't suppose they'd take a check?"

"Very unlikely," Harrah said as he opened the top drawer of his desk. "I half-expected we would be getting a call of this nature so I asked a clean $10 million be set aside. Frankly I'm surprised they only asked for five. Not very greedy are they?"

"It's not a good sign, sir." Hardesty shook his head. "Greedy people are easy to fool. Fools are unpredictable."

"Maybe," replied Harrah. "But for the moment we have to play this card. It's the only one we have."

"How about Hopkins?" Billingsley shook his head. "Do you still want us to, uh, make sure..."

"Don't worry about him yet. We know where to find him when we want to. This little ballet with the perpetrators has just begun and I'm not worried about a sharper with a Mercedes 210. We've only started this little dance and we don't know where it will lead. We can't afford to eliminate a player too early in the game."

Hardesty sensed a change in the wind. "I still say Hopkins is involved. Deeply involved. He was in a position to tip the thieves. He's still a key

Chapter 14

player. In fact, I'm surprised the thieves haven't said they want to use him as an intermediary."

"Oh, it's coming," said Harrah with a cruel smile. "I anticipate moves, like a chess player. We're going to have a few false starts and some testing, at least until the perps are sure we're serious. Then they'll bring up the name of Hopkins who is going to refuse to become involved and then, finally, relent and participate."

"Do we want him involved?" Billingsley drummed the desk.

"Right now we don't have a choice." Harrah stood up and, taking the cue, the two men stood as well. "We need the $10 million back. If we have to deal with scum-sucking pigs, so be it. At this moment, they are holding a very strong hand."

"Perhaps," Hardesty said as he pulled his suit jacket down over his bulbous belly. "But things could change awfully quickly."

"But not before five. That's when they're going to call back. In the meantime I want the two of you to go to the Federal Express Terminal at San Francisco International. Ten million in clean money came in – or is coming in. Make sure you get an armored car that doesn't stand out like a buffalo in a herd of goats. And stay in touch."

Chapter 15

Odd it was that a man should be sitting on a park bench beneath Rodin's Thinker at the Palace of Fine Arts on weekday afternoon in drizzling fog. But there he was, in a black plastic trench coat, braving the perils of a typical San Francisco afternoon of mist and drizzle and rain. Overhead the sky was a solid dark gray and the air had a wet smell.

The man was dressed for the weather. He wore field boots with deep canyons in the soles to allow rainwater to drain away quickly. Above the sheath of the boots and beneath the hem of the raincoat were three inches of Levi's blue jeans. He wore neoprene gloves, a favorite of skin and scuba divers and a sweatband held his hair in place beneath the black, broad-brimmed fisherman's hat which allowed the water to drain in rivulets onto his shoulders and back. He was smoking a cigar, the end of which he kept cupped beneath his left palm. His right hand was in his trench coat pocket. The only bit of light color was the man's silver beard and mustache, which could be distinguishable a block away.

But he wasn't on the bench long. As soon as Douglas Hopkins came running up, holding his black silk jacket collar up to keep the rain from working its way down his back, the man stood up. Hopkins wore no hat and his light blue pants were in the process of being plastered to his thighs. Even from a distance it was clear Hopkins' patent leather loafers would be saturated with water before he made it to the park bench.

"Are you going to stand around in the rain?"

"I hope not," Hopkins pointed toward his car. "Can't we sit in the car and talk?"

"Not a chance, Hopkins."

"Why not?"

"Because while we're standing here, I've got a bit of control. In your car, I don't know if I'm being bugged."

"Why would I bug you?"

"To save your ass. Look, Hopkins, the reason I'm not in any hoosegow is because I am very careful. Sitting in someone else's car is asking to be nailed. Nope. We'll take a walk."

Hopkins and the man in the black plastic rain jacket hop-scotched their way over and around the filling potholes in the gravel footpath. Hopkins dashed ahead and made a beeline for the entrance to the art gallery but was drawn alongside the building. The men walked under the false, concrete balcony and rounded the corner into the vaulted hallway. Here they were out of the rain but the wind coursing through the building channel was chilling.

"Let's make this quick."

Hopkins shook the water out of his shoes as he flexed his knees in the hallway as though he was running out of time to get to a bathroom. "I don't have any problem with doing this quickly."

"So far things have gone according to plan and we are still doing OK. Now comes the tricky part. Making the exchange. Why did you want to meet? The original deal was you were not to be personally involved. You're only in this for the cash, $1 million. We make the exchange, you get your cut and we disappear. Why do you want back in all of a sudden?"

"Too much is riding on this exchange. If it gets screwy, I'm the one holding the bag."

"Hopkins, you're the amateur here. You can't be trusted to think like a professional. Or act like one. Butt out. You've got a good alibi and will have a $1 million by nightfall. Not bad for an Ivy League dropout. All you have to do is stay clear. You'll get your cut."

Hopkins was still on edge. "It won't take long for Noonan to figure out I was the inside man. It's just a matter of time."

The man in the trench coat kicked unconsciously at the wet gravel. "So what? The man's got no proof."

"I'm the nervous type."

"No reason to be. And again, by midnight you'll be one million dollars richer and we'll be long gone. Any change now is going to screw up the works."

But Hopkins was obsessed. "There is a good chance English Petroleum is not going to like the idea of making the payment themselves. They're British, for God's sake. They don't do things the American way."

"Give me a break, Hopkins! They've been washing money for their drug friends in South America for a cracking plant in Bogota for years. They're going to be so happy to get their scrambled serial numbers back they're not going to bat an eye."

Hopkins pulled his collar tighter around his throat. Then he scuffed his feet like a frustrated child. "I'm just looking out for me. This entire exchange could go haywire."

"Hopkins, all you have to do is be around in the shadows when we make the final switch. You get your cash and we go. We shouldn't even be talking about this. I should not even be here! When we need to make the exchange we'll be in touch."

"How are you going to stay clear of Noonan? He's an unexpected twist. He works alone and could be anywhere. Maybe I should stay with him?"

"We've got him covered very well. Wherever he goes, we know. Don't spend your time worrying about him."

"Are you tailing him?"

"No. We don't need to."

"Are you sure you don't need me? After all, I . . ."

"Douglas! This is a very tricky time. You're out of the loop until we make the exchange! Stay public and keep your cell phone on. When we have to make the exchange, we'll call." Hopkins tried to say something but he was cut off again. "No! Whatever it is, No! Now let's go!"

Before Hopkins could respond, the man in the plastic trench coat moved away from the hallway and stepped into the rain. In the next instant the downpour filled his ears with the drumming sounds of raindrops on his hat. He made it to his car, an ivory Ford, without looking back. He made it out of his parking space in the near-empty parking lot without looking back either.

But he did look in the rear vision mirror when he came to a stop where the parking lot disgorged its flow out into the street. There, at the stop sign, he noticed one of the cars in the lot was slowly moving toward him. A questioning look crossed his face for an instant. He edged his head slightly sideways to sharpen the angle of his view in the rear vision mirror. From this vantage point he could see Douglas Hopkins walking dejectedly across the parking lot, oblivious to the two cars. When he returned his view to the car easing up behind him, he registered it was being driven by a black female. When he saw she was talking on a cellular phone, he hesitated for a moment before hitting his left-hand turn signal. Smiling, he spun the wheel and eased out of the lot, fumbling for his cellular phone in his chest pocket. He hit speed dial and put the phone to his ear.

"Yes." The line connected without a ring.

"I'm made."

"He's poison."

"Appears so."

"Describe."

"Purple Subaru station wagon. New, no plates. Hertz sticker in window. Driver a black female, about 35, 5 foot 10, athletic, brown shirt. Speaking on cell phone."

"Use Route Niner. Repeat, Niner. Recontact in 10." In the next instant the cellular went dead.

Chapter 16

Lt. Archibald Wu – Arch to his friends – picked up the body of the telephone and dragged it to a free desk in the back corner of the Property room. It really wasn't necessary because Wu shared the office with no one, but being sequestered in a corner gave him the feeling of being more private than in the center of the room.

"Where is he?" John's voice was as distinctive to Wu as it had been with the hostages.

"Midtown, Chinatown. I don't know exactly where."

"How long has he been there?"

"At least an hour. He appears to be walking around, not using a car."

"Stay on him. We don't want the old man messing anything up at the last minute. Keep a bead on him."

"Not a problem. Hopkins?"

"Poison now. Be ready to travel."

"Had my bags packed for a decade." The phone went dead.

Chapter 17

Harrah was at his desk when the call came in. The distinctive ring of his private phone purred rather than jingled. He gave the phone an annoyed look and then waited for a second ring. And a third. Halfway through the fourth ring he picked up the phone as if it were a tea pitcher. Without an octave of hesitancy in his voice he simply said, "Yes?"

"This is John."

"What a surprise, dear boy."

"Yeah. Do you have the money?"

"Of course."

"All $5 million."

"Naturally."

"Is it within reaching distance?"

"No, actually it's in an armored car. Do you have the $10 million within easy access?"

"Yes. Now I suggest one of your trusted employees should come to examine the $10 million and one of us will come and look over your $5 million."

"I don't like the suggestion at all," Harrah fiddled with the digital readout on his phone.

"Don't bother tracing this call, Mr. Harrah. I'm driving around the city with a disposable cellular so you won't be able to pinpoint me."

"It never crossed my mind."

"Of course not. Now, as I was saying. Have one of your trusted employees on the corner of 10th and Irving in 15 minutes. We'll make the people

The Matter of the Vanishing Greyhound

exchange there. We'll pick up your man; you pick up ours. Then both will go their separate ways."

"I'd rather not send my own man. I'll send Douglas Hopkins, the insurance agent who handles such details. He has access to the serial numbers."

"No, Mr. Harrah. One of your trusted employees, not an insurance agent."

"No honor among thieves?" Harrah shook his head sadly.

"You should know, sir. You'll be making a cool $5 million on the deal. Why would you want your insurance agent involved?"

"Just to see if he was."

"Ah! So you suspect if you gave him $5 million he'd just disappear."

"The possibility never crossed my mind."

John laughed. "Whoever said you English dogs don't have a sense of humor? Just send one of your trusted employees. We'll look at your money and you'll look at ours. When everything is hunky-dory, you will be called to make the final exchange. I wouldn't want any misunderstandings to crop up at the last minute."

"Won't be possible."

"No, it will be possible. No one is going to exchange this kind of money without some kind of assurance English Petroleum will leave us in the clear, old chap. You boys have a nasty reputation for sending hit squads out after people you find, shall we say, troublesome."

"Whatever you believe, true or otherwise, is fine with me. But I can assure you I will not be present at any exchange." Harrah was frozen at his desk. Though he appeared unperturbed by the call, there was nervous tick in his neck, immediately below his jawbone on the left. It throbbed visibly.

"No. No. Mr. Harrah, this is not some dime novel. This is a multi-million dollar exchange. Thieves surround us. What's to keep your cohort from pocketing the $10 million and saying he never got it? And what's to keep you from pocketing the $10 million and saying you never got it? With the serial numbers so scrambled, no one would ever know. Do you see my point?"

"Not really. Why would I take $10 million of English Petroleum's money?"

"Because it doesn't exist. You get your $10 million back and $10 million in insurance. Not a bad exchange. But the first $10 million is invisible. If it disappears, it's gone forever."

"I have no intention of being anywhere near any money when the exchange is made."

"Then we have nothing to talk about," John said and the phone went dead.

Chapter 18

"Where is he now?"

Lt. Wu looked over his shoulder, surveying the room. When he was satisfied no one was looking in his direction, he slid sideways on his desk chair to his computer screen. He booted up to the homing program and punched in a code number. When the computer screen cleared, it was a street map of San Francisco. Wu looked over his shoulder again and then punched in a three-digit number code followed by two letters and then three more numbers. In an instant, the screen showed a light near the corner of Stockton and Powell.

"He's still in Chinatown," Wu said into the phone as he hit the off switch on his computer. "Near the corner of Stockton and Powell. I don't have time to get an exact fix."

"Wasn't he there about an hour ago?"

"Yeah. Somewhere near there."

"What's he doing? Sightseeing? I thought he was supposed to be looking for us."

Wu pulled the telephone to the length of its wire and rolled his chair to the empty desk near the back of the room. "Look, John. I don't know what Noonan is doing and I don't care. As long as he stays as far away from us as possible until this is all over I could care less. You did lose your tail?"

"Piece of cake. Lost her south of the park."

"I hope so."

Chapter 19

Jerome Rasperson, his real name and usually followed by a sic. in parenthesis even after 19 years with the San Francisco Business-Herald, was not at all interested in what the police had to say about the strange robbery involving ten million dollars, a missing Greyhound bus and ten hostages. Here was a story crying for investigative journalism at its very best. And on an accelerated schedule. Never one to let a great story slip through his fingers, he was on the unfolding saga of the Butterfield-Fargo First National Bank robbery and kidnapping and disappearance of a Greyhound bus-like chrome on a trailer hitch. But, because of his background and experience, he took a different tack on the robbery than any other reporter in San Francisco.

From a physical perspective, Jerome Rasperson was hardly an unimposing character. He stood well over six feet and weighed enough to frighten heavyweight boxers. Thick of frame, he looked more like a gorilla than a bear and had a stringy, brown, unkempt beard making his face appear to be peeking out of a cave. The hair on his pate was short but refused to be tamed thus adding to his image as a wild man. While the rest of his colleagues wore clothes that fit like gloves, though some of them were oversized, Rasperson's hung loose but could not hide his massive body. He looked like a weight lifter even though he had not seen the inside of a gym since Spiro Agnew was Vice President.

As a Vietnam veteran, not of the press corps but the Army corps, he was not adverse to being under fire – political or sniper – and knew the best stories came not from press conferences but press confrontations. While the rest of the reporters were covering The Night of Vanishing Greyhound

Chapter 19

from the bars and briefing rooms of the San Francisco Police and Mayor's office, Rasperson was on the streets. This was where his resources were the most remunerative.

This was hardly a run-of-the-mill enterprise. Following the time-honored tradition of snitches, Rasperson used every connection he had with the San Francisco over and underworld, which were considerable as he had been a crime reporter for nearly two decades. While his stature in the crime reporting business was roundly stated to be based on fluke, accident, coincidence and luck, those in the legal establishment knew Rasperson maintained ties with the underworld primarily because he was considered a two-way street of information. He was intimate with the workings of the San Francisco Police and as such could barter, bargain and exchange favors and tidbits with snitches.

Even before the rest of the San Francisco press establishment began parking their BMWs the day of the robbery, Rasperson was on the street. Something about the theft intrigued him. As soon as the police frequency began babbling of a hostage situation on Monday at 10:30 a.m., he knew this was a big story.

Hostages?

At 10 a.m.?

Usually hostages in a bank job came when the thieves were caught redhanded in the bank with the police on the outside.

Second, his anonymous tip came from an unknown source.

Rasperson didn't have unknown sources.

On the street, no one knew anything. Nothing. Nada. Niento. Goose egg. Zip. It was as if Martians had landed to rob the bank.

By noon it was clear whoever was in the bank, Martians notwithstanding, was not local. They were also either very foolhardy or had planned meticulously. It also looked like an inside job. This particular branch of the Butterfield-Fargo was one of the newest offices yet it was in the worst possible location. It was situated in a neighborhood where the residents didn't know the difference between a certificate of deposit and an elephant molar. It had the standard security equipment but was not hooked into any overall security network grid even though such a network had been in operation at the other Butterfield-Fargo banks for several years. It was tiny yet, at the same time, had extensive banks of security deposit boxes. Since locals, in that kind of neighborhood, usu-

115

ally retained security deposit boxes Rasperson had mused, who would be using the boxes?

Taking advantage of the new computer network, he was able to hook into the indexing for the San Francisco Business-Herald and search for anything on Butterfield-Fargo First. Nothing was out of line. They were in good shape fiscally and were not involved in any risky financial ventures. Their stock was considered a good investment and their board of directors included some of the most financially secure men and women in San Francisco.

Then he got a list of names of the hostages from a friend who worked at Butterfield-Fargo and ran them through the linkup he had with the police computer and the public domain file operated by the State of California. He got another goose egg. Other than a few traffic tickets and a civil suit here and there, not one of the hostages had any kind of a record which would have raised eyebrows anywhere. Most of the hostages were buying cars and most of those loans were through Butterfield-Fargo. Three of the ten were buying homes, also funded by Butterfield-Fargo. One had a fishing license, none had a hunting license, one was an authorized gun dealer and four were voter registrars.

Given enough time he could have investigated the spouses and families of the hostages but a remote connection didn't seem likely. On the surface the hostages appeared to be just what they were: pawns. But what about the money? Why would someone take hostages at a bank operating in a crack house district? Did the bank have any money? And what about those security deposit boxes? So he ran a title search on the bank building itself. The building had been bought through a foreclosure sale two years previously from an insurance company, Capital Assurance and Fidelity, Inc., which still owned the property and rented it out to Butterfield-Fargo. They also insured the bank's deposits. When he called the insurance company, he was told the San Francisco representative, Douglas Hopkins, was at the bank. When asked for the number of the archives of Capital Assurance and Fidelity, he was told Hopkins handled all those matters. Rasperson thanked the man on the line and put in a call to the State of California Division of Insurance. They told him what he suspected, Capital Assurance and Fidelity, Inc. was a new, small company headquartered in San Francisco. They were a dwarf in the field, but there had been no complaints about their service.

Chapter 19

A bell went off in Rasperson's head and he went back to his newspaper network and the public domain file. This time he ran the name Douglas Hopkins and Capital Assurance and Fidelity, Inc. What he found was a bit more promising. Hopkins had appeared prominently in the social columns, but usually in the "also in attendance" sentences until about two years earlier when he had been credited with snagging a plum account with English Petroleum. Since then his fortunes had steadily been on the rise.

Rasperson ran Hopkins through the crime computer and came up with zip. The public access files gave him the license plate for Hopkins' Mercedes as well as the bank which financed it and his condo: Butterfield-Fargo First.

Back in the public access file and checking by date, Rasperson found once Hopkins picked up English Petroleum as a client he was mentioned with even greater frequency in the business section. His firm, "self-funded and self-owned" as he was wont to say in all interviews, began picking up clients with ease. But the clientele list was a strange mix of enterprises: auto wreckers, coffee shops, bars, taxi cab fleets, painters and roofers, building contractors, carpeting companies, video production firms, and two breweries. Behind English Petroleum, the largest firm represented by Hopkins had 35 employees; English Petroleum had close to 50,000 depending on how the economist wanted to make the count – and just in the Bay Area.

Running the business names associated with Hopkins, he discovered most of the firms were marginal operations. They were all long-time San Francisco businesses but none of them seemed to be particularly profitable. He ran the names of the businesses through the public access civil files. He discovered a ream of court cases involving every aspect of business malfeasance from price gouging to failure to repair when paid. Almost all of the businesses had been defendants. Taking whatever names he could find from the defendants' files, he ran these through the police computer. What he found was a rogues gallery of human cupidity. Fraud, price fixing, larceny, receiving stolen property, forgery, failure to pay court assessed fines and every aspect of collection violation were included along with a wide range of traffic violations.

Why was English Petroleum dealing with this kind of insurance company? Was there any connection between English Petroleum and the Butterfield-Fargo Bank being robbed? He answered the latter question with one phone call. Yes, English Petroleum had money in that particular branch of Butterfield-Fargo and it was cash: $10 million in cash, as a matter of fact. Was $10 million an unusual deposit? Well, his friend had replied, not really as English Petroleum had money in all the banks, often in large amounts and sometimes in cash.

But it was unusual because that particular bank was considered to be the Rikers Island of the chain.

If someone screwed up big time, they ended up there. How much cash was insured? The friend couldn't say offhand and promised to call back in half an hour. She was back in ten minutes and said the paperwork said the $10 million in cash was insured. Further, and of interest, English Petroleum had run six shipments of the same size through the Mission District Branch in the past two years.

It was all Rasperson needed. Even before the rest of the press began to queue up at the Butterfield-Fargo First for the initial press conference of the day, he was on scent. What could English Petroleum be doing with all the cash? It was too much to be used as payoffs – besides the fact payoffs, rebates, kickbacks and every other kind of monetary exchange in return for favors was illegal. Further, if the bank knew of the cash then the IRS had to know of it too and therefore the IRS knew whatever English Petroleum was doing.

So he placed a call to a friend in the IRS. Two hours later he got a strange answer. The IRS was aware English Petroleum was dealing with large amounts of cash but other than the fact the serial numbers were being reported; no one had ever asked what the money was to be used for. This wasn't unusual, he was told, because the IRS wasn't interested in how the money was being spent, just that all income was accounted for in tax returns. Since the IRS had the serial numbers of the bills, there was no reason to worry about illegal activity since the serial numbers could be traced.

Then Rasperson punched up English Petroleum in the Wall Street Journal on the Internet and spent the next three hours reading everything he could find. By midnight, long after the television reporters had gone to bed, he found a line in a short paragraph on the possibility English Petroleum was interested in building a hydrocarbon cracker in Corrialus del Santiago in Colombia. On a hunch he pulled out a world atlas and looked up Corrialus del Santiago and was not surprised to find it was not on the map; one didn't normally build hydrocarbon crackers in the center of populated areas. What was unusual was no one else in the oil industry was looking at doing anything in Colombia. Besides the obvious problem

Chapter 19

with the cocaine cartel there was ongoing violence in the streets and a general breakdown of law and order. After what had happened to Anaconda in Chile with Salvatore Allende, it should have been driven home to the multinationals it did not make good business sense to construct anything in areas that were politically unstable and the state of affairs in Colombia seemed to epitomize the term.

Could English Petroleum be buying political stability? Hardly likely. Not with $10 million here and there. The Sandinistas had drained the United States treasury to the tune of hundreds of millions of dollars and still lost. Could English Petroleum be using the cash to prop up the drug lords? This didn't seem likely either. He didn't know what the cocaine traffic amounted to but even $100 million seemed to be a drop in the bucket. Besides, wouldn't the IRS be watching the serial numbers if they came in from overseas? The first time the money showed up in an illegal shipment, English Petroleum would be on the hook.

But even if English Petroleum was using the money in the United States, what was it using the money for? With a simple bit of calculation work he figured even if there had been six shipments of $10 million apiece and the company had been slipping it out into circulation at the rate of $10,000 a month, it would take 6,000 months or 500 years to slip it into the market unseen. To launder so much money, it would take almost $250,000 a day in cash to get rid of the money within a year.

Since this made no sense, he attacked the problem backwards. Since the IRS didn't get snippy when he asked about English Petroleum he had to assume there was no ongoing investigation. This meant none of the bills associated with English Petroleum had ended up in an illegal transaction. Therefore either English Petroleum was legally using the money – a possibility which Jerome Rasperson, ace crime reporter, rejected out of hand – or they were illegally using the money overseas. But they could not be using the money illegally overseas if the IRS was involved. Which made no sense because if even one bill showed up in a drug money shipment, English Petroleum would have IRS agents going over their books line by line.

The only logical explanation was English Petroleum was using untraceable cash overseas, which meant they were laundering their money in the United States first. This clearly solved the problem of leaching the bills out one at a time into the market. Now it was just a matter of exchanging one bill for another one of an equal amount. Thirty businesses laundering

$25,000 a month each would just about cover the $10 million. They could probably do more. As the bills showed up in the banks they would be checked for their serial numbers. But since the bills were not on any kind of a "watch for" list, they would be accepted as legal tender, which they were. But why launder the bills?

Just before he went to bed, Rasperson picked up the chase of the Greyhound bus onto the Golden Gate Bridge. He had snorted with amusement as he went to sleep. You couldn't lose a Greyhound bus on the Golden Gate Bridge – even in the fog. It was a trick of illusion. The real story wasn't the Greyhound bus, the hostages or the safety deposit boxes. It was the $10 million. He knew he would have a clear field the next day because every other reporter in town would be following the Greyhound angle.

He was correct.

No one was following the critical lead. The next morning he took his 7 a.m. coffee in front of English Petroleum. It didn't surprise him there weren't any other reporters. After all, the reason his stories were unique was because he had such a different perspective on matters and it gave him an edge. He didn't think like other reporters.

He figured there were two angles to work, one was Douglas Hopkins and the other was English Petroleum. Douglas Hopkins was a story he could work at his leisure; English Petroleum was a here-and-now story. The core of the story was the money: English Petroleum's money. The answer, as far as Jerome Rasperson was concerned, was here. But there were 123 floors of "here" at English Petroleum.

Not sure of exactly what he was looking for, he decided to take a stab at the direct approach. He didn't know anyone who worked at English Petroleum so he didn't have an inside line. But he did know where their building was located and he did know what the regional vice president of English Petroleum looked like. He had seen his photograph in several of the news stories he had read the previous evening – not to mention on the billboards around the city. With a little bit of luck he could snag the man in the parking lot for a quick interview.

If you don't know what to do, the old adage went, beat the bushes and see if any snakes crawl out – and the biggest bush to beat in this particular case was English Petroleum. Maybe, with a few well-placed, leading questions, he could get a rise out of someone. Maybe the someone could be the regional vice president of English Petroleum himself. Who knew? Besides, he didn't have a better idea.

It was a good plan.

At least on paper it was a good plan.

But his logic was flawed.

He had intended to stand at the front entrance to ENPET, the English Petroleum monolith, and stop Harrah when he came through the front door with a leading question but it quickly became evident this plan would not work. Even arriving at ENPET early it looked as though there was a flood of personnel entering the building. There was no way he could spot Harrah in the crowd. Even if he could, there was no way he could snag the man for a quick question. So he moved into the building and stood by the elevators like he was waiting for someone, which he was.

But all he caught was a glimpse of Harrah as the Regional Vice President walked across the lobby. By the time Rasperson broke out of the crowd around the main elevator, Harrah was inside another elevator on the far side of the lobby.

But he went into the elevator alone.

For the next few minutes, no one else used the elevator. Clearly this was a private entrance and for Harrah alone.

Rasperson was about to leave in frustration when two men approached the private elevator. They stopped and conversed for a moment and then one of them pulled a phone out of a wall panel next to the elevator. A handful of seconds later the elevator door opened. The two men stepped inside and the elevator door shut.

What struck Rasperson as odd was the physical appearance of the two men. While Harrah looked every inch an executive, or a Lord as the newspapers insinuated was in his future, these two visitors were a Mutt and Jeff show. One was tall and lanky; the other was built like a bowling ball with legs.

Rasperson was still standing in the lobby, the last of the flood of workers ebbing around him, when a young man approached the private elevator. He too stood by the elevator door and used the telephone in the panel. Rasperson walked across the room as if it he were heading for the men's room to get a better look at the man.

This man was in his late 20s or early 30s, dressed like a yuppie right down to his polished deck shoes. He looked vaguely familiar and it was only after the elevator had swallowed the man did Rasperson realize who

The Matter of the Vanishing Greyhound

it was: Douglas Hopkins. He had also seen his photograph reproduced in an issue of the San Francisco Business Herald. Though the reproduction qualities were poor, Rasperson was pretty sure the man was Hopkins.

There was one way to find out. Rasperson went back to his car and hooked his laptop computer to his cellular phone. Then he punched up the State of California computer and slipped in using a code provided for him by an informant. Then he fed in Hopkins' name. The computer burped for 30 seconds and then spit out what he was looking for: Douglas Hopkins drove a black and silver Mercedes 210 – ("Of course!" Rasperson snickered to himself) – and gave its license plate. Then Rasperson put his Cherokee in motion and began searching the English Petroleum parking garage, floor-by-floor until he spotted the vehicle – just as Douglas Hopkins made a bee line for his car.

"Talk about luck!" Rasperson said to him as he followed the Mercedes out of the parking garage and on what could only be described as a wild trip across San Francisco, which made Mr. Toad's journey a leisurely jaunt. Hopkins went to a police storage yard in Hunter's Point and then, with three men following in a green Chevrolet, drove back uptown to a coffee shop on Market Street. When all four men went into the coffee shop, Rasperson parked his car a block away and dug a telephoto lens out of his trunk.

But his luck didn't hold.

Just as he was putting the bayonet onto the camera, Hopkins and the three other men came out onto the sidewalk. Rasperson only got one shot over the top of his trunk and only because Hopkins was facing the lens. The second shot wasn't any better but by then the man in the police uniform was walking away, his back to the camera. Rasperson had waited, hopeful at least one of the men would turn around but when it happened, they were moving too fast for him to get a good shot. One man dashed across the street and jumped into the green Chevrolet where the man in the police uniform was sitting. Before Rasperson could get a shot, the Chevrolet was gone. When he churned his camera back to the sidewalk, he got a shot of the back of Hopkins getting into his Mercedes and disappearing around the corner.

The only shot left was of the man who was standing alone on the sidewalk. So Rasperson took it.

Then he did the only thing he could. He followed the man who had been left on the sidewalk.

Chapter 20

By late afternoon it was clear to Captain Noonan he was having an exceptional day. He and Detective Smith had picked up Hopkins in front of his office and followed him as he wound his way through the city to the Palace of Fine Arts, Smith in a purple Subaru and Noonan following in a Rent-a-Clunker van. The moment Hopkins jumped out of his Mercedes and headed for the Palace building, Smith left the Subaru and joined Noonan in the van. Slowly they fed the license number of each car in the parking lot into the laptop computer connected by cell phone to the police computer. Every car except one matched. It was a mid-size Buick but the plates were for a Volkswagen Rabbit.

"Bingo!" Noonan had then handed Smith a homing device.

"What makes you think this car is the one?" she had asked.

"Because I need a break and this could be the only one I'm going to get."

"How long should I follow him?" Smith had asked.

"Until he tries to shake you," Noonan had replied with a smile. "Don't make it too easy for him. But don't lose me. I'm not the one with the homing device."

Smith had smiled then and now, three hours later, they were sitting in the front seat of the van with binoculars searching the facade of a majestic residence with a sweeping lawn at 1906 Ruef Street.

The Ruef Hill neighborhood had originally been built during the graft trials of the early years of the Twentieth Century. It had originally been an exclusive neighborhood, which, in those days, meant no "J" people, then the code for Japanese and Jew. Mayors, magnates and madams had lived in these homes and it was said their ghosts still walked the hallways and bedchambers of some of the structures. But over the years the homes had decayed to such an extent it was laughingly said the only thing falling faster into the Pacific Ocean than the City of San Francisco were property values on Ruef Hill. This may very well have been true. But Ruef Hill had a certain historical charm, which kept it from going the way of the Mission and Sunset districts. This was primarily because, as its name implied, it was on top of a hill too steep to allow any construction on the ramparts yet, on top, was flat enough and large enough to provide stable footing for two dozen homes.

Finally, when enough yuppies with a sense of history took a fancy to "The Hill," as it was called, the neighborhood was revitalized – thanks primarily to the low interest, federally-insured, state-provided, city-managed, historical preservation 25%-forgiven-after-five-years, loans. The quality of denizens went up. Historic reclamation of the "majestic monuments to San Francisco's past," as the paper described the ramshackle mansions, gave the neighborhood an ongoing face-lift. All manner of contractors, renovation architects and historians were in the neighborhood from dusk to dawn.

The house at 1906 Ruef Street was typical of the neighborhood. It had columns large enough to support the space shuttle all along a frontage, which could only be described as a combination of American Colonial and Victorian. A front lawn limped along 30 yards of frontage with alternating sheets of clover and dandelions.

The building came to an abrupt corner next to a greenhouse sharing the same frontage. From their vantage point, Noonan and Smith could see the house was as deep as it was wide – and two stories tall. There must have been a third floor of some kind because there were two gables on the roof front, one of them open. There appeared to be some kind of renovation underway as there was a section of the front of the house where metal frames were braced against the front walls. Ten feet up there was a narrow board walk the kind carpenters or painters would use.

In spite of the neighborhood, the building was hardly a cheery place. The wood shakes on the roof were splintery and black with patches of green mold hop-scotching as far as the greenhouse. A screen of pepper trees blocked any view of the next home. The front of the house was a dull gray with white windows and black trim, perfect for a funeral home, but the structure was not color-coordinated for the rest of the neighborhood, which sported an array of reds, greens and blues.

There was a three-car garage set at a right angle to the house. On a covered porch which stretched from the garage to the house, Noonan and Smith could see painting supplies scattered around what appeared to be piles of canvas spread cloths. A sign reading "Floor Season's Painting" leaned against the side of the garage, wedged between a ladder and a stack of paint cans. This seemed to fit with the framing along the front of the structure.

"What can you tell me about this address?" Noonan lowered his binoculars until they were hanging around his neck by their leather strap.

"Let's see, 1906 Ruef. It's legit as far as I can tell." Smith looked up from her laptop. "It was bought ten years ago by Elsie and Jonathan Hutchings for $250,000. Valuation is now $573,000. No indication of any sale recently. She paused for a moment while she pulled up the police computer, "neither of them have any record of trouble with the police, at least back to 1965, as far as our records go back on computer."

"Anything in the public domain file?" Noonan pulled a pen from his pocket and scribbled the names down in his notebook.

"Just a second. Yeah, three law suits, plaintiffs all three. Two are for non-payment of rent and the third was a libel suit."

"Who was the libel suit against?"

"A magazine, the San Francisco *Tattler*. One of our local tabloids You know, dirt, dirt, dirt. If it's printed in the Tattler, it's not true."

"Did they win?"

"I can't tell from here."

"It's a docket we may have to check. What year was the case?"

"This year."

"Good! I like this cyberspace world better and better. Now, unless our little pigeon has found the homing device, this is the end of the road. The roost, so to speak."

"Do you want me to check the garage? It's the only place where he could have hidden the car."

"Not yet. I don't want to spook the man. Besides, if this really is the roost, there's got to be someone watching. I've got a better idea. See if you can find some neighbors and talk to them. Who are the Hutchings anyway?"

"Are you sure you want me to ask?" Smith pointed to her face as though to say "Hey! I'm black, remember?"

"Is there a problem with being black in San Francisco?"

"Not really but this is not exactly an integrated neighborhood. The only blacks you're going to find around here are little metal ones on the lawns with horse rings."

"You might be surprised. This is San Francisco, remember? The most multi-ethnic city on the West Coast."

Smith gave him an irritating look. "I'm betting every multi-ethnic person up here does gardening or laundry."

She was wrong.

The first doorbell she rang produced a short Japanese woman in a sweat shirt which looked more like a painter's drop cloth than a piece of clothing. The sweat shirt read "Nikko's Gallery," a good indication it may very well have been used as a palette.

She wore baggy jeans and water buffalo sandals. Armed with a glass of white wine in one hand and a pair of reading glasses and book in the other, the woman looked at Smith's badge and then said, "Well. It's about time. What are we paying our taxes for if you people can't get here on time?"

"Excuse me?"

"You're with the police aren't you?" She made the word "police" sound like it was a disease, the same emphasis would be placed on "used car salesman," "insurance agent" or "candidate for Congress." When Smith nodded, the woman continued. "I just can't believe you people take so long to respond to citizens. I made the call this morning and here it is, what, 3:30. Did I pull you away from a doughnut shop?"

"Actually, Ma'am, I not here as the result of a call to headquarters."

"Well, officer, we pay quite a healthy amount of property taxes to live in this neighborhood and a large chunk of the mill rate goes for police protection. Now if you are not going to provide top flight service to the neighborhoods who chip in the largest chunk of your budget, there really isn't much use in us paying taxes is there? Every time I go downtown I see cops on every block. But when we report a peeping tom in the neighborhood, I guess we have to wait until someone gets their throat slit while they're asleep before anyone responds. What's your name officer?"

"Smith. Detective Smith. Where is this peeping tom you called about?"

"Isn't it a little late to cover someone's back end?"

"It's never too late to stop someone from getting murdered in their sleep, Ma'am. Now where is this intruder?"

"He's hiding in the bushes up the street, at the top of the hill overlooking the Hutchings house. He was sitting in a new Cherokee down the hill for a while but I guess he's got to do his peeping with a camera. He's been there since I woke up. He has a long scraggly beard."

"The Hutchings house? The one across the street, with the framework for the painting?"

"Yes. Jonathan and Elsie spend every July in Montana. Jonathan loves to fish for trout and Elsie collects burls and mushrooms for her artwork. She's an excellent artist. We feature some of her pieces in our . . ."

"Yes, Ma'am." Detective Smith pulled out a notebook and a stubby pencil. "The Hutchings go to Montana every July. So the house has been empty? Is anyone living in the house?"

"Four or five, actually, but I don't know who they are. There's at least one couple, a man and a pregnant woman. Probably not married, you know how those things are these days?" The woman gave Smith a leer.

"No, Ma'am. I'm married."

"Good for you," the woman replied and then pointed across the street with her wine glass. "The painting only started last week, Friday, I think. Four men put up the frames but I haven't seen a whole lot of work. There were quite a bit of goings-on over the weekend but it's quiet now."

"So there's no one there now?"

"One person. I saw him drive in about half an hour ago. He locked his car in the garage – a bit strange for this neighborhood. We really don't have a lot of cars stolen from around here. Now, what are you going to do about the peeping tom?"

"Where is the man in question right now?"

"Like I said before, Officer" – and the word officer was said with a sliding sarcasm just apparent enough to indicate derision but was not offensive enough to be worthy of a comeback – "he's hiding in the bushes near the top of the hill." The Japanese woman pointed across her front yard to a figure barely visible at the crest of a small knoll surrounded with brush.

"How did you ever spot him?"

"In this neighborhood we watch out for our neighbors. I'm a member of Neighborhood Watch. I see something suspicious, I report it."

"Well, he can't really be a vagrant if he drove here in a $20,000 car. You said the Cherokee was new, didn't you?" The woman nodded.

"Do you have a pair of binoculars?" Smith shaded her eyes to see if she could spot the Cherokee.

"Sort of. That's how I spotted him." She stepped back inside the doorway and reached through a bead curtain, the strings clacking as her shoulder broke the plain of the beads. She pawed her way across a piece of furniture in the dim interior. When she returned she had a bronze telescope with a stand. "I like the spyglass, myself. Can you use one of these?"

"I think so." Smith gave a half smirk and focused on the Cherokee at the top of the knoll. It was a newer model, silver and gray, with tinted windows. Then she shifted her gaze to the white male hulking in the bushes. She could not distinguish his face because he was glued to a Hasselblad with a telephoto lens. From the angle of the lens he appeared to be watching a back window of the Hutchings House.

The license plate to the Cherokee was obscured by a bush so Smith stepped sideways on the porch and up onto a cinder block. But she still couldn't see the plate.

"I tried that too," the woman said behind her. "I finally crawled through the bush and took a look. In the rain, too. The things I do for Neighborhood Watch."

"Did you write it down?"

"Of course."

Again came the sound of the bead curtain being swept aside.

Smith put down the spyglass and exchanged it with the woman for a piece of paper.

"I recorded this for our next meeting of Neighborhood Watch. You never know what might be important."

"You are correct." Smith looked at the plate number and shrugged. "I'll see what I can do."

"I certainly hope so." The woman closed the door so quickly behind her she almost cut the end of her statement off.

Back in the Rent-a-Clunker, Smith punched up the license plate.

"Did you find out anything?" Noonan was relaxing in the van, his eyes riveted to the house with the painting scaffolding.

"Yeah. This neighborhood's integrated. Uh-oh."

"I don't like the sound of that." Noonan tore his eyes away from the house. "Tell me everything you know for a fact before you said Uh-oh."

"Which do you want first, the good news or the bad news?"

"Let's try all the news."

Chapter 21

Hopkins was piling rather than packing a quartet of red leather suitcases, the smallest one just large enough to accommodate a grand piano. He had stowed his suits and shoes in one, all of them, and was stuffing the others full of a wide variety of household objects. Just as he was deciding what else to include, his bedroom telephone rang. He ignored the initial rings as he set his bags against the wainscot of his living room where they stood like a lobster quadrille.

"Yeah?"

"Douglas? This is Robert Harrah. We've got a problem."

Chapter 22

"What does Sandersonville, North Carolina, have to do with the San Francisco Police?" That was Rasperson's first question as he poured himself into the back of the Rent-a-Clunker and was sitting on the timber slats of the cargo hold, his jeans scraping on the broken knot holes whenever he shifted his weight.

"Let's just say I was invited," Noonan replied. "What are you doing here?"

Rasperson looked at Noonan for a moment and then arrogantly dug into his pocket and pulled out a notebook and a battered chewed 19 cent plastic ball-point. "What's it to you?"

"Look, Rasperson," Smith reached back from the passenger's seat and flicked Rasperson's notebook closed with the fingers of her right hand. "What we have here is known as a moment of cooperation. Now, if you want to play the hard-nosed reporter, I'll run your butt downtown on an Obstruction of Justice charge and let you sit in a cell for 48 hours, just long enough for this story to finish. On the other hand, if you want to cooperate with us until this is over then you'll get a great story, pick up another inside contact at the Police Department and get a bird's eye view of the biggest law and order bust in San Francisco since the Great Graft Trials."

Rasperson looked at Smith and then at Noonan. Noonan just shook his head, "I'm just a visitor to your fair city, son, but I'm sure she can run your behind in for suspicion of something, even if it isn't obstruction of justice."

Rasperson put his notebook away. "OK. What do you want to know?"

"Everything," said Noonan. "Let's start with the moment you first heard of the robbery."

Chapter 23

"Where is he now?"

Wu punched up the homing template on his computer screen as he looked over his shoulder at the office door through which he could see blue uniforms scurrying around in the Property room. "He's at the Saint Francis Hotel. The old man's given up on us!"

"Good. We're getting close to finished now. Keep an eye on him, say every 15 minutes. If he moves, let me know."

"On the cell?"

"Yeah. I'll be out of here in a dozen minutes. By the by, Hopkins is back in." John said it offhandedly, as if it meant nothing.

"Not good. Not bad. Be careful. He's not a professional."

"He's worth $7 million."

"Seven? I thought it was five." Wu leaned forward unconsciously, his hand cupping the phone cradle.

"It was. Harrah wasn't very cooperative. It's going to cost him an extra two."

"Will he pay?"

"He'd better."

There was silence at both ends of the line for a moment. Then Wu said, "I'll be in touch if the old man moves."

131

Chapter 24

Harrah was buttoning his black leather trench coat while Billingsley and Hardesty checked their weapons.

"Are you still carrying a fly prick?" Billingsley pointed his Colt .45 at Hardesty's .38. "You get a big man he's not going to do much more than burp when you hit him."

"Depends on where you hit him, don't it, Gov?"

"Not if you're carrying this," Billingsley waved the .45.

"Don't get too enthusiastic yet." Harrah shook his head at the display of firepower. "It's still a long, long way to Tipperary. Anything could happen."

"And Hopkins?" Billingsley looked at Harrah. "From the moment we walk out this door it's going to be very hairy. This curtain is going to come down fast and we might not have time to talk in private again." He chambered a round, checked to make sure the safety was off and then slipped the weapon beneath his belt at the small of his back.

"Our first concern is our money, the original $10 million. The money takes top priority. We secure the money – and I mean all the way back to a safe location. Then we worry about Hopkins. I don't want gun play until the money is secured. None. Do both of you understand my words?"

Billingsley and Hardesty nodded.

"After the money is secured we'll have another talk. But I don't want anyone killed, hurt or injured in any way; anything can be linked back to us. We don't need the bad publicity."

"So we just let Hopkins get away with plucking $10 million of our money out from under our noses?" Hardesty bent his head forward and looked at Harrah over the top of his glasses, his bald pate shining under the overhead lights like the moon.

"It's 5 o'clock now. This should be wrapped up by 7. Who knows what might happen at 8?"

Chapter 25

If there was anything positive to be said about the six hours Greenleaf and the others spent in the abandoned butcher's shop it was everyone got a stinging introduction to group therapy. It started with everyone talking about their kids and spouses. Then the conversation went foul and everyone began to beef about their current conditions. Several hostages sat stony-faced as the remaining hostages talked about some of their experiences, none of them at the bank. Over the course of the past few hours they all learned Freesia had spent one night of the previous week in a car with an old boyfriend at Beluga Point and "Nothing happened, I swear it," she said. "He's got a girlfriend."

"Then what were you doing with him out there?" asked Greenleaf.

"We were just talking," Freesia had replied.

Most of the men snickered and none of the women believed her.

Several of the women talked about their children and one man told a story of how he had become lost on a fishing trip in Eastern Washington and almost been eaten by a bear. The branch manager told a story about his first day on the job as branch manager and everyone listened politely with "This is bull" written all over their faces.

The talk at up about two hours. The following five hours were spent in virtual silence with most of the hostages either sitting on the metal chairs staring at each other or walking the room looking over each wall as if this was the first time they had seen it and were testing it for weakness.

Chapter 26

Hopkins was sitting in the Ryder truck six car spaces from the corner of 10th and Irving when he saw the ivory Ford pass him and turn the corner. Hopkins stayed in the truck as instructed, the windshield wipers squeegeeing through the sheet of rainwater coursing down the windshield. When he saw his contact walking along the sidewalk back toward him, he turned on the Ryder's lights.

"Our contact is here," Hopkins said to Billingsley who was sitting in the back of the Ryder truck smoking a cigarette smelling like burning spice. "Better pull your hat down, it's really wet out there."

"Don't pull anything funny, Hopkins." Billingsley pulled out his .45 and showed it to Hopkins. "One mistake and you go down, as you American chaps say."

"Put the gun away, Billingsley," his partner said. "You might hurt yourself. Now why don't you be a real good boy and go with the nice man."

Billingsley rose from the empty floor where he was sitting and walked to the back of the truck. The vehicle lurched as he opened the cargo doors and stepped onto the bumper and then the gutter.

"Don't close the door!" Hopkins shouted after him. "I'm going to have company."

Billingsley left the door open. A moment later Hopkins saw Billingsley and the perp John converge in the gloom of the wet evening. They talked for a moment and then John indicated with his right arm Billingsley should walk to the corner. He did and disappeared around the edge of the pharmacy window. John walked past the Ryder truck to the rear door.

The back of the Ryder truck shook as someone got in the back.

Chapter 27

"How's it hangin'?" Hopkins looked at John.

John stepped into the cargo bay and closed the door behind him. "Turn off the lights, you idiot."

Hopkins turned off the interior lights and John moved to the front of the truck. But he didn't sit in the dead man's seat. He squatted down in the cargo area below the window level and nodded his head. "Let's go."

Chapter 28

"I stared out of the front of the van window at the two men walking. "I've been sitting in a van so long I feel like I'm a cop," Rasperson looked toward the driveway on Ruef Avenue. "Where did the thin guy come from?"

"Have you seen him before?" Noonan was peering at the pair through binoculars.

"Yeah. I saw him and a guy built like a bowling ball go up to Harrah's office."

"How do you know they were going to Harrah's office?" Smith looked over her right shoulder at Rasperson in the cargo area.

"He's got a private elevator to his office. He's the only one who uses it. I saw him go up and then a little later, these two hoods went up."

"What makes you think they're hoods?"

"Because only four people went up to the Harrah's office the day after the robbery: Harrah, Hopkins, this guy and his partner. It was at seven in the morning let me quickly add. Why do I think they're hoods? Because that's the way I'd do business. The day after a robbery of my $10 mill I'd have my heavyweights looking into the situation right away."

"Good guess," Smith said. "Any idea that they are?"

"Not a one."

"We've been running on luck all afternoon," Smith said.

"No," said Noonan. "We've been running on good police work all afternoon, Detective. This is how crimes are solved. Luck doesn't have a lot to do with it." Noonan put his binoculars down and dropped them into a duffel bag on the floor. "It's too dark to use these. Now, don't lose those two. If I'm right, they're going to lead us directly to the English Petroleum's $10 million."

Chapter 29

The speaker came on so unexpectedly the hostages jumped in unison.
"This will be your last transfer."
The voice came over a loud voice was not that of John.
"Listen very carefully. There have been major complications we are endeavoring to work out right now. Once again, let me make it as clear as glass, we expect no trouble from you and will tolerate none. In five minutes the front door will be opened and you will queue up again. When you hear a knock on the door, walk directly into the vehicle in front of you. Do not look to the left or right. Just walk straight ahead. So far we have had no problems, don't be a problem now. If all is well you should be home by midnight, alive and well with a great story for your children."
"What if we don't have children?" Freesia yelled.
But there must not have been any wiring to take incoming questions as the voice continued as though no statement had been made from the hostages.
"It's been a long day and it is almost over. Let's not ruin such a splendid relationship by any last-minute stupidity."

Chapter 30

"Where is he now?"
"Still at the St. Francis Hotel. Where are you?"
"Enroute."
"Keep me informed. I've got my tickets and bags."
"Over and out."

Chapter 31

"Now let's see our seven million." John waved a gun at Hopkins indicating he should pull away from the curb.

"Put the gun away, John. It makes me nervous."

"Having to deal with you makes me nervous, Hopkins. This wasn't in the plan."

"I'm not real pleased at being here either."

"It's not what you said this afternoon, Douglas. I don't like the way things have been twisting. This smells like a double-cross."

John took a look over the leading edge of the dashboard and then hunkered down again. He tapped Hopkins in the ribs with his pistol without saying anything. But the action didn't require any vocabulary.

"Give me a break, John. What am I going to get out of a double-cross? You get out of town, and I get a million. You get caught, I get zip. What have I got to gain by turning you in?"

"Seven million dollars, Hopkins. You think we're stupid, don't you? Clever little plan it is too. English Petroleum gets their 10 million, we get seven and a-maz-ing-ly we get picked up by the constabulary. No honor among thieves, eh?"

"How does it get me seven million dollars?"

"Because the seven million doesn't exist. English Petroleum won't claim it. If they do they'll have to explain what they were doing with it. Even if there isn't a law against having seven million dollars, the IRS is going to wonder about it. No. English Petroleum isn't going to squeal over $7 million. Ergo, once we make the switch, you don't need us. You've got seven million reasons to turn us in."

Chapter 31

"Well, if you're so sure I'm going to double-cross you, why are you dealing with me?"

"Because I have no choice." John paused for a moment and then waved the gun at Hopkins. "But I can assure you if there is any hanky-panky I will not hesitate to use this. Period. If it looks like we go to prison, you go to the graveyard."

"But if you go to prison, I go too."

"You're a cockroach, Hopkins. A cockroach will survive a nuclear war. No, you're the kind of slime who would stack our bodies one on top of the other to reach a pizza counter. You just do exactly what you're told. Now. Let's go."

Chapter 32

Chief Thayer was sitting at his desk rolling a pyramidal ruler over the sea of paperwork inundating his blotter. (A friend who was an engineer once told him this was actually called a triangular scale but, as Chief Thayer had said to his friend, what did engineers know about rulers? The Chief had chuckled at his own pun but the engineer needed an explanation.)

Centermost was a pile of photographs of the Butterfield-Fargo First, the three bungee cords dangling from the underside of the Golden Gate Bridge, and the newest collection, the Hunter's Point Salvage Yard. He flipped some of the photographs over with the ruler and then turned them back over as if doing so would recombine the visual images and reveal a meaningful clue. But if it did any good, he could not see it.

With a sigh he picked up his cellular phone and started to dial. Then he stopped, shook his head sadly, and set his phone down. He pawed through the paper piles again, started to reach for the cellular phone when it buzzed.

"Heinz?"

"You're supposed to say, 'I told you never to call me at the office.'"

"Boy, how funny, Heinz. Ha. Ha. Now, where are you?"

"I'm in the back of a Rent-a-Clunker van following an ivory Ford with one of your perps inside sitting with a hit man from English Petroleum. Where should I be?"

"I don't need any jokes, Heinz. Daylight has faded and you said we'd have this wrapped up tonight."

Chapter 32

"We've still got six hours of nighttime, George. Now, I need you to do some things for me."

"Am I going to want to do this, Heinz? Tell me I'm going to like this."

"Of course you're going to like it, George. Just don't ask me why. Now, I want you to get three or four unmarked cars ready to go at a moment's notice. Do it personally, not on the radio. We don't want our inside man to know what is happening."

"Have you found the hostages?" He was on the edge of ecstatic.

"Not yet. Just give me a few more hours. I assure you all the hostages are alive and well. But I don't know where they are at this moment. But we will know very soon."

"OK. When do I get to make a bust?"

"In about an hour or so if I'm correct. Now, I want you to send a man to my room at the St. Francis Hotel and pack up my clothes. Then I want you to have my bags taken to the San Francisco International Airport. Check me in on the midnight flight to Anchorage, Alaska. I'm going to want to wear my leather jacket when I go so will you make sure it's hanging up in the courtesy lounge closet? I don't want it stolen so will you make sure it's watched?"

"You seem to care a lot about the jacket."

"I do. Will you take care of it?"

"Sure. Anything else?"

"Not yet. Just be ready to roll when I give you the word."

"I'll be waiting." The Chief paused for a moment. "I've got a tidbit of news for you but I'm not sure what good it will do either of us. We got a call from Butterfield-Fargo. English Petroleum requested and received $10 million in cash. It came in – are you ready for this – on a pallet on a Federal Express plane."

"I believe it."

"We checked with the air cargo people who confirmed English Petroleum had picked up the shipment. It was placed in an armored car and driven into San Francisco. No destination was listed. I don't like this, Heinz. Now I've got another ten million to keep an eye on."

"Are you tailing the armored car?"

"Of course. I've got a car on it because I feel nervous this week."

"Good job, George. I hope you're not using the police radio."

"No, no. Everyone I trust is using cellular. I trust those men, which is why I'm using them. Actually, one of them is a woman."

"Bully for Affirmative Action." Noonan's voice was broken by static for a moment and then came back on line. "...payoff money so don't lose it. Let's hope none of the good guys does anything foolish. We have to catch everyone red-handed."

"Not a problem." Chief Thayer picked up his pyramidal ruler and tapped on a pile of photographs. "To bring you up to speed on what is happening on this end, the armored car stopped at a warehouse near the University of California San Francisco Medical School and the drivers unloaded what appeared to be ten crates. My people said the armored car was loaded with crates but they only unloaded ten. One person stayed behind and the rest drove away in the armored truck."

"There's only one person with the ten crates at the warehouse?"

"As near as my people could tell."

"Where are your people now?"

"Two are following the armored truck. Detective Caleb stayed at the warehouse."

"OK. Don't do anything until I tell you to do so. We're following the other end of the payoff. We want to catch all the rats in the same trap."

"You know, even for a desk jockey like me, this is getting really exciting." Chief Thayer chuckled.

"Don't take any tranquilizers yet." Noonan snapped his cell phone off before the Chief could reply.

Chapter 33

Wu passed the word immediately. He surreptitiously punched up the homing device, an action he was performing every five or six minutes. When he saw the bug had moved he got on the phone immediately.

"He's on the move."

"Where is he now?" John's voice came over the phone line.

"South. Way south. Appears to be heading for San Francisco International."

"Hot damn! The old man's leaving town!"

"Could be."

"Stay in touch."

Then the phone went dead in Wu's hand.

Chapter 34

John snapped his cellular phone shut. "Your man is on the move, Hopkins – the Detective from North Carolina. He's on the move. But he's heading south. I certainly hope this isn't a trick of yours?"

"Hey! I don't even know what you're talking about."

"You'd better not. Now. Let's go get the other truck."

Hopkins headed east along the edge of Golden Gate Park and then turned left to run along the width of the park panhandle. Following John's direction, he meandered through the Sunset District with John keeping a sharp eye on both outside rear vision mirrors. Finally he had Hopkins pull Out from a small vacant lot next to a Chinese grocery store and a laundromat where a van was waiting, its engine running.

"Pull in here." John jammed his gun into Hopkins' ribs for emphasis.

Hopkins pulled in and stopped. John stood up in the Ryder truck and wedged his way to the passenger side door. He stopped for a moment on the passenger seat and stuffed his pistol in his waistband.

"This has been a bad night for smooth sailing. Let's not have any problems, Douglas. We're on a tight schedule as it is." He slid the front door of the truck open and stepped into the vacant lot. A few steps later he was in the van. The tail lights snapped on as the vehicle lurched backward.

Hopkins put the truck in reverse and moved back out onto the street. Then he put the truck in first and moved forward, the van following closely behind. He drove down to the end of the street and then went through a series of bizarre turns and finally ended up heading south. Twice he saw the headlights of the van flashing behind him but he kept driving south,

Chapter 34

putting more and more distance between himself and the van. Finally he got a call on his cell phone.

"What the heck are you doing," snapped John. "Trying to lose us?"

"Yeah, well, let's just say the rules of the game have changed, John." Hopkins rubbed his ribs where John had been jamming the gun. "Five minutes ago I was satisfied to participate with you. Now, with your attitude and pistol, well, let's just say you don't inspire confidence."

"Exactly what do you mean?" John's voice was malevolent.

"What I mean is I can no longer trust you, John. What's to keep you and the rest from ever giving me my $1 million? I went to a great deal of trouble and personal risk to set up this caper and now, just as we are about to win big time through my efforts, you're talking about a double-cross."

"What!"

"Sure. I've taken all the risks here. Set up the whole deal and all you did was sit in a bank for a few hours and break open security deposit boxes with a hammer and chisel. I took all the risks. If this is successful, as I am sure it will be, you get to walk away with $7 million cash, everything from the safety deposit boxes and leave me holding the bag. I get no money and a prison term."

"We wouldn't do a thing like that."

"Oh, yes you would, John. The gun proves it. So, since everyone seems to be going after their own cash, I'm going to make certain there isn't any double-cross. This is going to take a bit longer than anticipated and John, you are not going to like this one bit."

Chapter 35

Harrah took the call on his personal line. "This had better be good, Hopkins. You're running out of time."

There was the roar of static on the cell phone and finally Hopkins's voice could be heard plainly. "A bit of a problem. It seems the hostages have disappeared."

"What?" Harrah rose from his desk chair in surprise.

"The contact, the man who got into the truck told me the hostages had disappeared. The couple who was guarding them missed a rendezvous. Then they called and said they wanted another million or they'd kill the hostages. Right now no one knows where they are."

"You're kidding." Harrah smiled. "Is this your idea of a shakedown, Douglas? Squeeze an extra million out of English Petroleum. You certainly are greedy."

"This is a very dangerous situation, Mr. Harrah." Hopkins' voice had the plaintive plea of a desperate man. "This is completely out of my hands. The two say unless they get an extra million they're going to blow the hostages up with a car bomb. These people are crazy! I swear it!"

"How do I know this isn't a bluff, Douglas?"

"Why would I bluff you? I'm not the one getting the $1 million. I'm not even the one they trust to deliver it. Besides, what does English Petroleum care? You're covered for $10 million. But if those hostages go up in smoke, you're going to have more scrutiny than you can stand, if you know what I mean."

Harrah pulled the phone back from his ear. He pressed it against his chest and looked pensively out the window at the pitch black night beyond. He held his stare for a good thirty seconds. Then he pulled the phone away from his chest.

"...there? Are you there? Hello? Hello?"

"Yes, I'm here." Harrah slowly spun his chair sideways as he reached for his sandalwood humidor on the shelf behind his desk. "Now, Douglas, I'm going to give you some instructions on where to find an extra million dollars. But, Douglas, don't forget – and I am serious – I want the original $10 million by midnight."

"Yeah, I remember." Hopkins' voice sounded strained. "But right now I'm worried about staying out of the gas chamber."

Chapter 36

"We've got a tight schedule to keep." He looked sideways at what the heck are you doing now?" John's voice was irritated. "We haven't got time to screw around on personal business."

"Yeah, yeah, yeah," said Hopkins over the cell phone. "But right now we're going to a warehouse and get my one million dollars."

"What?"

"Are you having a hard time hearing? We're going to play this my way. We're going to get my million first. We're going to make an initial withdrawal, so to speak, and then we're going to drop off my million in a safe location. Then we'll finish the deal."

"You can't be serious! Our schedule is too tight for any cowboy stuff!" The driver looked at John with panic in his eyes. John shook his head reassuringly and mouthed, "Keep cool."

Hopkins' voice was steady. "There is no honor among thieves, John. You said so yourself. I no longer trust you. We'll just take a side trip. If you don't like it, pull alongside and shoot me now. Then you'll never get a dime."

There was silence in the van for a long moment, the driver looking at John with questioning eyes. After bouncing over some cobblestones, the van hit a stretch of smooth pavement and it was quiet enough to hear a conspiracy breaking.

"Douglas, we can work this out, can't we?"

"Sit back and enjoy the ride, John. The faster we get my one million, the faster you get your seven."

Chapter 37

"I feel this is not one of my better days," Cheri Molk said as she settled into the same plastic chair she had been in all morning. "I feel like I'm being dragged from pillar to post and beyond. How am I going to explain this to my boyfriend?"

"You're still alive, aren't you?" Greenleaf nodded toward the rest of the hostages. "We all are. Count your lucky stars. It could be worse."

Chapter 38

Billingsley spent 15 minutes lying on the back floor of the ivory Ford, his pelvis bouncing on the drive shaft housing, which ran down the center of the floorboard. His host had covered him with an army blanket, comforter and then a threat. "First time you poke your nose out from under the blanket, I'll shoot it off. Got it?"

Billingsley said something the driver took to be in the affirmative so the vehicle had lurched into traffic. It was the last contact Billingsley had with San Francisco until the car pulled to a stop. He started to rise, like a ghost of wool and nylon piling, until he felt the prod of metal on his head.

"Not so fast, my man. You stay down."

Billingsley settled back onto the floor and listened to the drone of the idling engine. Then he heard what sounded like a garage door going up. The Ford inched forward and then its engine shut off. This was followed by the sound of a garage door going down behind him. There was silence for a second and then the shroud of blanket and comforter was pulled off his head and the rear door to the Ford jerked open.

"Outside, my man," came the booming voice of the driver.

When Billingsley came up for air, his eyes opened and then immediately snapped shut before the withering blast of a light directly in his eyes. He brought his hands up to protect his face. With his hands pressed against his eyes he was helpless.

Two pairs of hands pulled him out of the back of the Ford and jerked him erect. When he was finally able to stand, another pair patted him down, pulling the .45 out of the small of his back.

Chapter 38

"You're a bad boy for bringing a gun with you. You can have the gun back, but we'll keep the clip, OK?" The voice boomed close to Billingsley's ear and he felt his .45 being slipped into the small of his back. He heard the slide click back and the ping of a shell hitting the cement floor.

With his fists still in his eyes, Billingsley was half-pulled, half-walked a dozen steps and then spun around.

"You can open your eyes now." The only sound Billingsley heard other than the soft whine of the floodlights was the scraping of canvas being pulled back. "You just be sure you spend all your time looking straight ahead at the money, not behind the lights at us, got it?"

Billingsley grunted and when he opened his eyes he was facing a sea of money, 1,000 bricks of $100 bills. They were stacked on a single pallet, three feet high. There was no question these were the bills from English Petroleum because the bills were clearly not new. Each of the bills on top of each of the bricks had a slightly different discoloration. Some were fairly new, others appeared to have been dredged from the Bay and dried in a kiln.

"There's no reason to match serial numbers so you'll just have to check each of the bricks to make sure we didn't pull out $100 bills and slip in newspaper."

Someone to Billingsley's left, just out of his line of sight, handed him a brick of bills whose paper band had been sliced. The pair of hands fanned the bills to show they were all hundreds. Then the hundreds were tossed onto the pallet of bricks. "Take all the time you want in examining the goods."

"Now you know I don't have the time to examine all of the bricks."

"Then you'll just have to take our word for it. There are 1,000 bricks here, each with $10,000. If you don't want to check them, fine. It's up to you."

"How do I know you won't cheat me?"

"Because if we did, you'd have a contract out on us."

"You've been reading too many espionage novels."

There was general laughter behind Billingsley. Then the same voice came back, booming next to his ear. "Listen, man. English Petroleum does whatever it pleases here, in Africa, Colombia, Panama, anywhere. No, if the company thought it was at risk, there would be a hit out. So we play it safe. We get our insurance. Then we say good-bye."

"What kind of insurance are we talking about?"

"Now I'm glad you asked me. As soon as you're satisfied these bills are legitimate – and as soon as our man informs us the $7 million is available – we're going to make a little exchange. But the Regional Vice President of Pacific Rim Operations for English Petroleum is going to be here when the exchange is made."

"Why?"

"Because we want the man on film. So he can't say he never got the $10 million. As long as we've got the tape, no one can say we double-crossed the company. And English Petroleum can't press charges."

"Suppose he won't come."

"He's already said he would. If he doesn't, he doesn't get this $10 million. We're very sure he doesn't want any complications. Now, take your time and examine to your heart's content."

Billingsley asked for a knife, which was tossed onto the top of the bricks. Carefully he picked his way onto the stacks of money and began picking up random bricks, slicing them open and checking their contents. He spent 20 minutes crawling around on the bricks, pulling up random bricks to examine. After he had opened two dozen of them, several from the bottom of the piles, he appeared satisfied.

"OK. I'm satisfied enough. Toss me some kind of a bag to keep these loose bills from spilling.

A black plastic garbage bag arched out of the darkness and landed next to him. Billingsley gathered up the loose bills and stuffed them into the bag.

"OK. What's next?"

"We wait until we hear from our man. You can sit on the bricks. Good boy. Who else can say they sat on $10 million?"

"Richard Nixon?"

Chapter 39

"Caleb's high-pitched voice melded with the static on the cell phone."
"Step into the clear, Caleb. I can't hear you." Chief Thayer pulled his telephone cradle as far as he could as he walked toward his closed office door. "OK. Who showed up?"

There was another moment of static, which suddenly went to snow and then clear. "...ry, Chief. You're are not going to believe who just came by!"

"Surprise me."

"Hopkins! He pulled up in a Ryder truck with two guys following in a van behind him. They all walked into the warehouse and talked with the guard for a moment and then the guard got on Hopkins' cellular. They talked for a moment and then Hopkins and the two men took three of those boxes the armored truck had dropped off."

"He did what?!"

"He picked up three of those boxes, put them in a Ryder truck and both vehicles drove away."

"They just drove away?"

"Yup. Do you want the license numbers?"

"Absolutely." The Chief scratched down the numbers as Caleb gave them. "Which way did they head?"

"South."

"Stay alert, Detective. Things are coming down fast."

"Yes, Sir."

Caleb signed off and Chief Thayer pushed speed dial for Noonan. "You're not going to believe this."

"Compared to what? A Greyhound bus disappearing off the Golden Gate Bridge?"

"Very funny. Hopkins and a van just showed up at a warehouse where English Petroleum had some crates stored. They took three of them."

There was silence on the other end of the Cybernet for a moment. "Three of them? You mean he took three crates?"

"Correct," Chief Thayer repeated. "Three of them. Put them in a Ryder truck and headed south with the van following."

"South?"

"South. Where are you?"

"Well, there's not a lot north of here. I presume there's no way to follow him."

"Sorry. My men are spread so thin there's nothing I can do now."

"Too bad. Hopkins is a loose wire. Where are you?"

"We're sitting up the hill from the house, about thirty yards from where we found our pigeon earlier today. 1906 Ruef and you'd better get out your taxicab map because you're going to be coming here soon. But not yet, George. I want all the rats here before we spring the trap. Right now there's at least one English Petroleum man inside. I'm assuming the $10 million is here but unless we catch everyone red-handed we've got nothing. We can see light under the bottom of the garage door so I'm assuming our birds are inside the garage."

"When can I send in the cavalry?"

"When all the rats are here. Hopkins is going to have to come back and, of course, I want to catch that son of a sea cook George Harrah."

"You don't really believe he's going to show up?!"

"Oh, he's going to show up all right and I want to catch him red-handed. Don't you?"

The Chief was about to say something but stopped. He looked around the room suspiciously and then said, "Yeah. I guess I do."

Chapter 40

Greenleaf and the others were leaning starboard when suddenly the vehicle came to a sudden stop. It was odd because one moment they were moving slowly and the next there was a screeching which ran the length of the cargo hold, like Paul Bunyan was dragging his fingernails across a blackboard. The vehicle jiggled as it came to rest and there were voices outside, arguing wildly.

"Just one word and I will flood this van with gas." The voice from the butcher's shop came over the intercom into the back. "Just one word."

No one inside said a word but outside they could hear voices of outrage.

Chapter 41

John was beside himself with rage. "We don't have time for this, Douglas! You are putting everything in jeopardy!"

Hopkins dumped the last of the boxes into the trunk of his Mercedes 210. Slamming the trunk he gave it a shake to make sure it didn't re-open. "Look, John. I didn't plan to double-cross anyone. I still don't. But I don't trust you. At all."

"Douglas! You're putting $7 million at risk! Not to mention putting us all at risk of jail time. For what? A million dollars when it's coming to you anyway?"

Hopkins just smiled and backed the Mercedes into his parking stall. He hit the security alarm button and the distinctive chirp told him it was working. Then he closed the garage door to his stall and walked back to the Ryder truck. "So much for trust, John."

John jumped back in the van and the pair of vehicles pulled out of the condominium parking lot. As soon as they were out on the streets, Hopkins punched up John's cell phone. "This caper is falling apart rapidly, John. When you start double-crossing your partner there's no room for sympathy. I'm covering myself. My money comes first. Now we pick up the rest of the money. Let's get this finished."

John was not happy. "Let's not forget we've got a long way to go before the end of the night, Douglas. Be very careful, Douglas, because, Douglas, you never know what might happen, Douglas."

"You've said Douglas four times now, John. I got the message. Now let me give you one. Mess with me and you will end up on a slab."

Chapter 42

The deep booming voice in the garage broke the silence. "Where the heck have you been?"

Billingsley started to look over his shoulder into the darkness behind him but someone gave him a prod and he averted his eyes. He had been sitting on the $10 million for close to 45 minutes now and from his squirming about it was clear he was uncomfortable. It was like sitting on a cement floor, he had commented, and one of the perps had responded it was the most expensive cement floor he would ever sit on.

"Look, guys. This is getting ridiculous. Let's get this over with." Billingsley stretched his legs and wiggled his toes as best he could. "I've got other things to do, places to go, people to see."

"Stow it, buster." The voice was of a cultured woman trying to be tough. It floated out of the darkness like a scent of perfume in a cattle yard.

There was silence for a moment and then the booming voice was back. "We've had a bit of a difficulty with your man Hopkins."

"He's not my man Hopkins. He's an insurance agent."

"Nevertheless there has been a problem. It seems Hopkins is freelancing."

"What a surprise." There was a moment of silence. Then there was the sound of a round being chambered. "Hey! I'm not responsible for Hopkins."

"Apparently no one is. We are running on a very tight schedule so I do not want any misunderstandings as to what is going to happen here. Any slip ups and I assure you there will be drastic consequences for all concerned. And I am referring not only to this $10 million but to the hostages as well. Do you get my drift?"

"Fine. When is something going to happen?"

"As soon as Hopkins and our man examine the $7 million. Then things will move quickly."

"Well, I hope it's soon. My butt's killing me." Billingsley stretched again. "Life's a bummer."

"Cut the talk."

Where is Hopkins?" Billingsley asked.

"He's just picked up the seven mill. Now. Let me tell you how this is going to play out, hot shot. Right now there are two vehicles coming this direction. One is the Ryder truck your people rented. The other is the armored car with the seven mill. You call your main man now. When he gets here, we make the switch."

"My main man, as you call him, is not going to be very happy."

"He knows the score."

"He is still not going to be very happy. When do I get in touch with him?"

A cellular phone was tossed out of the darkness. It bounced on the bricks of $100 bills and skittered toward Billingsley. "Right now. Then you slide the phone back to me. I'll give him directions as he drives."

Chapter 43

Noonan snapped his cellular phone shut and stuck it back in his pocket. He turned to Smith and Rasperson and smiled. "The money's been picked up. The bad boys are on their way here. Now, Jerome, things are going to get very hairy very fast."

Smith looked at Noonan imploringly. "Any news of the hostages?"

Noonan shook his head. "I wouldn't worry about it. They are going to make an appearance very quickly. The perps are about to get their money which means they are going to release the hostages in some way to draw the maximum amount of attention you can get on a slow news night.

Rasperson, who was still sitting in the back of the van, slowly got up and brushed his pants off with his hands. "Now, it's all fine and good but it's time for me to go to work. I was getting so used to sitting here. Thank goodness something is about to happen." Then he started to shuffle toward the back of the van.

"Where are you going?" Smith asked.

Rasperson looked at her in surprise. "I'm a reporter, remember? It's been a fun-filled afternoon, folks but, frankly, it hasn't been very productive. Now, however, it is about to be productive. I've got to get my camera gear. I want a shot of the thieves standing beside $10 million in stolen currency."

"You think they're going to let you get a shot?" Noonan turned slowly and looked at Rasperson. "How old are you, son?"

"Thirty-five, why?"

"Because I'm over sixty. I've been around quite a bit and the around I've been has been dealing with some of the slipperiest people in

America. I don't want to tell you how to do your job but I can give you some advice and that advice is to be subtle when you deal with men like Harrah and Hopkins."

"Why should I give a darn?"

Noonan gently rubbed the fingertips of his right hand on his forehead. Then he looked up at the ceiling and stared long enough until it appeared he was counting the rivets. "Didn't you say you were in Vietnam?"

"Yeah, so?"

"Did you trust the white mice?"

"Not a one."

"Well, it's the same way here. When the bad boys show up there's going to be $10 million of dirty money sitting on the floor of a garage, two heavies from English Petroleum and four or five bad guys who took ten hostages from the bank. Then there is the very real possibility there's probably an inside man in the Police Department. We don't really know who else is going to be in the garage in five minutes. But there is going to be another seven million dollars in an armored car. Do you think anyone is going to have any misgivings about murder when it comes to $17 million?"

"But I'm a reporter."

Smith didn't have any problem at all understanding what Rasperson was being told. So she snapped at Rasperson. "What he's telling you, newspaper boy, is those men in there will kill you to keep this transaction secret."

"Who's going to kill me with the police there?" Rasperson shook his head and chuckled.

Noonan snapped his fingers to draw the reporter's attention. "Jerome, right now I don't trust the San Francisco Police. There's a mole somewhere and I don't know who it is. Neither does the Chief. We're not using the police band radios because he and I aren't sure who we can trust. That's why we're using the cell phones. Now, if I walk in there and the inside man is part of the team, I'm dead and so is Detective Smith. There are just too many unknowns right now."

Rasperson was silent for a moment. "So what you're telling me is not to cover this story?"

Noonan smiled. "Oh, no. What I'm telling you is to stay away from the garage until lots of police get here. Like we said, things are going to be very dicey for about ten minutes."

"You really think someone in there may try to kill you?" Rasperson was incredulous, as though it was the first time he had thought of it.

Chapter 43

Smith gave me a strange look. "You know, Jerome, until this moment I had a lot of respect for you. Vietnam vet, a crime reporter who consistently got it right, good man on the computer to beat the police to a solid lead, but now I'm not so sure. Every morning I wake up I know I might be in a hospital before nightfall. It's part of my job. My husband knows it and my three kids do too. Now, here we are about to crack the biggest crime in a decade with $17 million in cash on the loose and 10 hostages in the balance and you think this is going to be a cakewalk? Sorry, Charlie. When the buzzards gather," she indicated Noonan and herself, "the two of us are going to walk down there and confront the thieves and try to stall for time until the troops get here. And you think you're going to walk in there with a camera and snap people's photos?! Where are your brains?"

Rasperson thought about it for a moment and then scratched his head. Leaning back he propped his feet against the van and settled against an empty crate. "You have a better idea?"

"Not really," Smith said. "Except you'll be in the way when shooting starts. It's going to be hard enough taking care of myself let alone a civilian."

"I've been in combat. I know what to do when bullets start to fly. So you want me to sit out the biggest story of my career?"

"No." Noonan stretched a bit. "Use the telephoto lens you keep talking about. Hunker down in the bushes again. Snap pictures of everyone coming and going. It keeps you out of harm's way and, at the same time, gives you a photo essay you can use even if things go smoothly."

"If they don't?"

"Then you can call 911."

"How very heartening."

"Jerome," Noonan nodded toward Smith. "She and I are paid to be targets. It's our job. We're going into a lion's den and those people in there are not going to be happy campers. Anything could set them off. Right on the top of the list is a newspaper reporter with a camera, got me?"

"Yeah, but I . . ."

"Make your decision fast, Jerome." Noonan looked out the front window of the van as Smith pulled on his sleeve. "Faster yet. I'd say the Bentley Flying Spur means the biggest pigeon we could possibly nail has just arrived."

A car turned into the driveway of 1906 Ruef half a block away and the street lights momentarily illuminated the vehicle.

"The license plate EP makes it a sure bet. Now, to make the group complete, all we need is Hopkins and the armored car."

Rasperson shrugged resignation. "OK. I'll be the fly on the wall with the telephoto lens even though there isn't a wall for me to be the fly on. Give me a couple of minutes to get to my Cherokee and pull my gear out. Then you just be sure the garage door gets opened wide otherwise I don't have a chance of getting any shots."

"Not a problem," Noonan smiled for the first time in hours. "Two more people in there and the garage is going to have to have its own zip code."

Chapter 44

Douglas Hopkins was driving the Ryder up Van Ness when the armored car ahead of him made a left on Clay. As soon as they made the turn, Hopkins received a call on his cellular.

"OK, here's where we part company, Douglas. We can settle any differences later. Make a right on Sacramento and proceed around Lafayette Park and then go to the Ruef address. You are not to follow me any further. With any luck no one will find the van until tomorrow morning."

"Yeah, we'll talk about it later."

"Right. But for the moment, follow the plan. Proceed to Divisidero and make a left, heading for the University of California. But wait to be contacted by cell phone. There might actually be someone in the garage who doesn't know you're the inside man."

"Yeah," said Hopkins' snidely into his cell phone. "I'm not worried about me. I'm worried about you. You do know you've got a tail."

"No kidding?" John's voice came over the Cybernet with a confident boom. "Well, we'll just have to do something about that, won't we?"

Chapter 45

"Where is he?"

Wu glanced at the computer screen. "Still at San Francisco International. He hasn't moved in an hour."

"If he does..."

"Yeah, I know. Call."

Chapter 46

The strong voice whispered over the intercom, "Not a peep."
There were some voices outside the vehicle which continued for a few seconds and then faded. All was silent for 10 seconds and then the truck lurched to life again. It inched forward, the scraping continuing for a fraction of a second and then stopped. The truck advanced, rolled slowly over a large bump and then slowly rumbled onto smooth pavement.

"I'll bet we took a corner too sharply. Probably took out a tree," the security guard from Butterfield-Fargo said. "I guess the new guy isn't used to the rig."

"Well, he'd better learn fast," said Cheri Molk. "I'd hate to end up locked in the back of a truck all night."

"Would that be more fun than a butcher's shop all day?" Greenleaf asked humorously and several people laughed.

Then the truck took another corner a bit too sharply. The starboard wheels hit what was probably the curb and the entire side was airborne for a split second. It came down hard and the port side bounced, its wheels clearly off the ground.

Chapter 47

Chief Thayer got his call seconds after the Ryder truck and the armored vehicle parted company.

"Which one do I follow?"

"Follow the money! The armored car! We're pretty sure where the Ryder is going. Follow the money!"

"Yes, sir."

"He says to follow the armored car."

"That won't be hard."

"Just don't lose him."

"How can you lose an armored car in San Francisco?"

Master of the Impossible Crime

Chapter 48

As Rasperson maneuvered his way through the shrubbery, Noonan and Smith prepared to advance on the garage. Smith pulled her .38 from the small of her back and clicked the cylinder open. After checking the loads, she replaced the pistol and then pulled a .25 caliber out of a holster on her right ankle.

"You certainly come loaded." Noonan smiled as he opened the cell phone.

"We don't know what's going to happen in there. Now, I assume you're calling for backup. This is not going to be a picnic."

Noonan hit speed dial. "Right you are. At times like this, I'll need all the friends I can get." He smiled at Smith and then broke into conversation on the phone. "Chief. Yes, it's time for backup. What?"

Noonan was silent for a moment as he listened intently on his cell phone. Then he looked up at Smith. Covering the mouthpiece, he said, "Hopkins and the armored car split up. There is an unmarked car following the armored van but Hopkins is on his own. The Chief is assuming he is on his way here."

"I sure hope he is." Smith looked out the front window of the van nervously.

"The Ryder truck is empty so it's only reasonable he's on his way here. I think it's about time we close in."

Noonan looked at his cell phone again and spoke into the equipment. "Chief. We're on our way in. Yes, we are armed. Rather, Smith is armed. No, I don't expect any trouble. You have the address, right? Good. Harrah is here now so I'm sure he'll talk rather than fight."

Noonan was silent for a moment and then confirmed the address of the house. As Detective Smith listened, Noonan gave the layout of the house and the garage. Smith let her hand stray to her pistol. Noonan closed the phone and turned to Smith. "OK, Detective. Time to earn those big bucks."

They both went out different doors of the van, Smith on the driver's side and Noonan from the passenger side. It was still raining outside and the cool, wet staccato of the rain drops on their heads was a relief from the stuffy interior of the van. All around them was the wet smell of the flowers and the pungent odor of some kind of brush. Noonan couldn't see Rasperson but he knew wherever he was, there was a telephoto lens focused at the garage.

Noonan and Smith casually walked across the rain-slickened street and up onto the sidewalk on the far side of the street from where the van was hidden. Down the cement slab they walked, a house and a half and then cut across the wet lawn to the corner of the house at 1906 Ruef. If anyone was watching they didn't give the alarm, or at least there was no movement discernible from Noonan and Smith's vantage point. Smith pulled her pistol free and looked at Noonan.

"You didn't bring a gun?!" Smith's whisper was harsh and incredulous.

"I hate to get powder burns on my cuffs. They are so hard to get out. Let's go." He pointed toward the garage with his head. "Shall we make our entrance?"

Smith nodded and the two of them stepped under the scaffolding and moved through a tarp tunnel parallel to the house. When they were less than a dozen feet from the side door of the garage, Noonan broke out from the protection of the house and walked quickly to the door. He had his hand on the knob and was turning it just as Smith caught up with him. He twisted the wet knob in his and hand and pushed the door open. Stepping inside in front of Smith and her leveled revolver, he made his entrance. Behind him, Smith stood in the doorway, obligingly holding the door wide open allowing the light inside to spill out onto the wet lawn and walkway.

Master of the Impossible Crime

Chapter 49

If the driver of the armored van was aware of the fact he was being tailed, his driving gave no indication he was aware of the unmarked car at his back door. But it was clear he was trying to be as difficult as possible to follow. Staying well below the speed limit, he wound his way through the city streets, double backing once and even stopping for 60 seconds twice in parking lots.

During the whole time the two detectives in the shadow vehicle were able to maintain their distance and surveillance without much difficulty. The only time the detectives became concerned was when the van went down Lombard Street. Once into the brickwork there was no way they could stay far behind and maintain any reasonable visual contact with the truck. But luck was with them because it was early enough there were other cars on the street, tourists from the license plates, and though they were two cars back, they could keep the van in sight the entire time.

The armored car zigzagged for another few minutes and then, after some strange maneuvers through a pair of parking lots connected by an alley, headed due west. From Fell to Kezar to Third to Parnasses the van drove without any bizarre actions. It passed the University of California San Francisco and then made a left on 14th. Halfway up the block it began to pick up speed and, four car lengths back, the tailing vehicle did the same.

The men had no inkling of any problem until the ancient Dodge Comet suddenly jetted out of a driveway on the left-hand side of the street. One moment the tailing car was leisurely driving behind the armored van and the next it was slamming on its brakes to avoid a collision. The unmarked car slipped to a stop but not before smashing into the passenger side of the Comet. There was a sickening crunch as the two cars met followed by the unrelenting high pitched whine of a horn in which its on switch had been permanently jammed in the open position.

As the two detectives watched helplessly, the armored van made a left on Kirkham and disappeared. Before they could get out of their car, a man came running down the stairs of the apartment above the garage from which the car had emerged. When he helped the driver out, it was clear she was gravid.

And she was hysterical.

Chapter 50

Rasperson wasn't sure what it was he was getting on film. In fact, he wasn't sure he was getting anything at all. The rain wasn't pelting but it was still making his job miserable. Huddling in the bushes hunched behind a tripod 20 yards back from the garage, he was praying he would be able to get a usable shot.

At least one.

All he needed was one.

But he was prepared. In addition to the 300 mm, 2.8 lens with 6400 ASA high-speed film he also had a second camera with a 500 mm lens. Whatever he got was going to be grainy. He also had the camera set on automatic and was using a power drive, two tactics he hated under normal circumstances – but there was not much normal about tonight.

The trick, he decided was getting as many quick shots as he could rather than good ones. When the side door opened he was going to have less than a second to get a shot. He had to be prepared. If he so much as blinked he might miss getting the Pulitzer Prize for Photographic Journalism.

A split second before Noonan entered the side door of the garage, Rasperson's finger was on the power drive. Taking a deep breath he held it to keep the mist of his breath from clouding any picture. Then he pushed the switch.

He was sure he had three frames of blackness and two of Noonan silhouetted in the doorway. But the next six were a blessing. Detective Smith held the door long enough for him to photographically blast into the room. On the first two he caught the back of a man turning toward the door. He had a full profile for the next shot and then a side profile of a second person, this one with a shotgun. Detective Smith was pulled inside and the door clicked shut.

"Thank you, Lord!" Rasperson let his breath out. "Three and six is nine. 36 less nine is 28. 28 shots left."

The reporter shuffled his feet in the mud and rotated his shoulders to drive the stiffness away. His breath clouded and obscured his vision for a moment. Still he stared through the SLR, afraid to move. Occasionally he flicked the dust cover more out of habit than necessity. If any rainwater fell, he didn't know because he is eye was glued to the garage doors at 1906 Ruef.

One instant the garage was simply a bank of three doors, wet with rain and dark with brown paint surrounded by a lawn that was black and set off by the pale ivory of the cement walkway and driveway. In the next instant the entire front of the structure erupted into light. One of the garage doors went up and an ivory colored Ford exploded out of the driveway. Rasperson got one shot, probably blurred, of the driver's face illuminated by the lights of the garage. At the same moment, through the lighted interior of the garage, he could see the back of a person as he or she disappeared out a door that opened onto the steep hillside of the house.

Rasperson's finger was on the automatic as the Ford momentarily cut his vision of the garage doors. When the car passed, he could see the side door to the garage was now open wide and he could distinguish three figures dashing around the near side of the house. One toppled a can of paint as he, or she, passed and a pale liquid spread across the now-illuminated lawn and walkway like honey on a table. There was a moment of silence and then, distantly, he heard the sound of motorcycles being started.

Rasperson cursed himself for missing the shot. But still he stayed in a crouch. Something told him it was not all over yet. Noonan, Smith, Harrah and at least one person from English Petroleum were still in the garage. "How many shots have I taken," he asked himself. "Seven? Nine?

Nineteen left.

What's going on in there?"

He didn't have long to wait.

Chapter 51

"You're working kind of late, aren't you?"

Wu looked up from his computer at the blue uniform in the doorway. "Yeah. I've got some work to get done. Helluva thing to have to do, work late."

"Well, it won't happen after you get married."

"Right. Right. Tell me after I get back from my honeymoon! Three fun-filled weeks in Hawaii." He leered suggestively and then waved haphazardly at the Hawaiian travel poster on his wall. Then he turned his attention back to the computer screen.

"Enjoy! I'll see you when you get back."

Wu waited until he was sure he was alone. Then he looked surreptitiously over his shoulder.

He was alone.

With precision he pulled up the homing map. The solitary flashing light at the San Francisco International Airport warmed his heart. He smiled.

But he didn't smile long.

The phone rang.

"Wu."

"Now," came the voice over the phone. "Now."

Wu hung up the phone. His fingers danced over the buttons and he cleared the board and killed the template. RAM swallowed and then he brought the homing screen up again. The flashing light at the airport was gone. Wu ran the mouse to exit and, two seconds later, hit the power button.

In 30 seconds he was on the street outside Police Headquarters.

Moments later he was crawling into the back of a delivery van and scrambling over seven million dollars in $100 bills in crates marked "chili." The last he saw of Police Headquarters was the red aviation warning light on top of the communications tower overlooking the Civic Center. Then the cargo doors of the van closed.

Chapter 52

After taking several minutes of verbal abuse from the pregnant woman's husband, the two officers were able to make contact with Chief Thayer to say they had lost track of the armored car. While they were talking on the radio, the husband helped his wife back up the stairs into the house above the garage. Two minutes later, when the officers went upstairs to get the names of the couple, no one answered their knocks. Through the front window the two officers saw the unit was empty.

From the front porch they could also see all the way through the kitchen to an open window situated next to an empty refrigerator.

When they reported into headquarters they were informed the Dodge Comet driven by the pregnant woman was stolen.

Chapter 53

Chief Thayer turned onto Older Avenue and split his entourage. He and the lead would enter Ruef Street while the next two cars would proceed only as far as the corner of Older and Ruef where they would block the cul de sac. The last car would proceed around to the Spreckels Parkway where they would block anyone coming down the slope from the back of 1906 Ruef.

The map showed a short walkway and the Chief had made it clear to his men he wanted the back door closed before he went in the front. Two minutes behind them was SWAT, one of the few times when blues went in before the hardware boys.

With clockwork precision the San Francisco Police took 1906 Ruef. Spilling out of their cars the men grabbed critical locations around the garage. Three patrolmen took positions on their bellies, shotguns leveled at garage doors. Two patrolwomen were sweeping around to the blind side of the garage while a team with drawn pistols was hunching through the painting scaffolding and tip-toeing through the spilled paint.

Chief Thayer, behind the front door of his patrol car, was bellowing threats over the microphone in his car when the middle garage door was slowly raised. Inside, clearly lit by the glare of the naked bulbs, were Harrah, Billingsley and Hardesty standing around what appeared to be a pallet of bricks. Noonan and Smith were standing at the edge of the garage door hauling on chains slowly raising the plated door.

Chapter 54

"Here we go!"

Rasperson switched the automatic camera drive off and took the photographs manually. "18, 17, 16 … 3, 2," and the camera jammed. Quickly he popped one camera off the tripod and bolted the other one down. It took him an instant to focus and then he started snapping again, "36, 35, turn a little bit, just a bit, Thank you, 34, 33".

By frame 30 the blue uniforms obscured the view, but he kept snapping. He only stopped at 21 when the garage door came down again. Then he reloaded the first camera.

"This ain't over yet 'cause the fat lady hasn't sung yet."

Chapter 55

After what seemed a lifetime, the truck suddenly braked violently and then took a left turn. For a moment the centrifugal force strained to pull Greenleaf out of her seat and then, when it abated, she was slammed back into her chair and against the wall. Now the ride was smooth and the truck slowed almost to a crawl. The noise of traffic disappeared and only the staccato of wheels on the cobblestone streets could be heard.

As the truck slowed even further, the new voice came over the intercom. "Your journey is just about completed, my friends. As long as there is no difficulty on your part, there is no danger. And I repeat, as long as there is no difficulty. Momentarily you are going to be leaving the vehicle and entering a building. We will be pulling this vehicle inside the building where it will be pitch black. While I will be wearing night vision equipment, you will be, as they say, as blind as bats. Just because it is dark, however, do not believe I cannot see what you are doing. And I will be armed."

Just as the speaker took a breath, the truck slowed to a crawl and then came to a stop. There was a grinding of gears, the transmission of the panel truck screaming in agony as its direction of travel reversed. Greenleaf was now pulled toward the front of the truck as it backed up. The truck traveled a dozen yards and then stopped. The engine idled and the truck rocked as someone got out, the door slamming.

Almost immediately there was the faint sound of a large garage door being raised. The truck rocked again as the driver got back into the cab. Again the vehicle was reversed, only to stop within 10 or 15 feet and gently tapped something solid. The truck shook again as the driver got out and, once again, there was the sound of a garage door. This time the sound of

Chapter 55

the door was punctuated with a slam indicating it had come down and met with the pavement. But this time the driver did not return to the cab.

"This will be your last transfer," the voice came back over the intercom. "In a moment I will flick off the lights in the vehicle and open the rear doors. You are to move forward slowly. The back of the truck is buttressed up against a loading dock so you should raise your feet a little as you step out of the truck. Though you will not be able to see it, there is a hallway directly in front of you. Once you are in the hallway, feel your way back to the last door. Open it and go inside. Don't worry about any of the other doors; they are all locked. And, once again, remember, I have night vision goggles on and I assure you if there is any hanky-panky not one of you will reach the last door alive. Now, please rise and stand in a line. Put your hands on the shoulders of the person in front of you."

There was a general rumbling of feet as the hostages stood. Suddenly the lights went out and instantaneously the back door to the van popped open. The rush of fresh air washed over the hostages and chased away much of the stench of the van.

"Move! Move! Move!" There was a tapping on the side of the van as the hostages were urged forward.

Greenleaf, her hands on the shoulders of the assistant branch manager, waited for him to move. When he took a step forward, she did as well. Behind her she could feel the rest of the line moving forward. In the pitch darkness she slowly shuffled forward, her toes gently probing the darkness for the loading dock. When the Assistant Branch Manager took a step up, she followed suit and felt the line behind her doing so as well.

Shifting her weight onto the loading dock, she felt the solid surface beneath her feet, clearly different from the springy bed of the cargo vehicle. The crunch of her feet on the loading dock told her she was walking on concrete. She felt rather than saw she had entered a hallway when the sound of her shoes told her she was on a slick tile or linoleum surface. Her hands still on the shoulders of the assistant branch manager, she moved forward.

After progressing a dozen steps into the hallway, Greenleaf was startled by the slamming of a massive door somewhere behind them. Then, muffled as though through a wall, came the sound of a large door being raised and the cough of a truck engine being started.

"Which door am I supposed to enter?" The voice of the assistant branch manager boomed in the darkness as Greenleaf felt him reach to his right and begin feeling for a wall.

There was no response. The only sound was the muffled slam of a heavy door.

"Hey!"

Still there was only silence.

"Hey, you!" Still silence.

Chapter 56

By the time Douglas Hopkins pulled up to 1906 Ruef, the area was littered with police cars. Harrah's Bentley was boxed in by a SWAT van and the lawns were awash with police officers, their bright badges sparkling in the headlights of the police vehicles as they stood around outside of the garage. No one seemed poised for action even though quite a few of the men and women in uniform were carrying shotguns at the ready.

As Hopkins pulled into the open driveway, two men in flak jackets held up their hands in a motion to indicate he should stop his car. Their uniforms were slick from the rain. He pulled to a stop and one of the men came around to the driver's side window. Hopkins rolled down his window.

"Who are you? And please keep your hands on the top of the steering wheel, sir."

"Douglas Hopkins. Capital Assurance and Fidelity, Inc. I was told to be here with a Ryder truck by my client. What's going on here?"

The man with the shotgun didn't bat an eye. "Will you please open up the back of the truck for us?"

"Is there something wrong?" Hopkins turned toward the window and his hands slid on the steering wheel. This caused the remaining policeman in front of the truck to react nervously.

"Please keep your hands on the top of the steering wheel, sir. Now. I would like to check the contents of the truck."

"There's nothing in the truck."

"Yes, sir. But I'd still like to have a look. You see, I'm from Missouri." Hopkins nodded his head. "How am I supposed to get the key to the back

The Matter of the Vanishing Greyhound

off the keyring when it's in the ignition without taking my hands off the steering wheel?"

"Very slowly, sir. Very slowly." He nodded to the shotgun-wielding SWAT troop and then returned his gaze to Hopkins. "Now, sir. Very slowly reach one hand down and turn the engine off. Then, toss the key ring out the window."

Slowly Hopkins reached down and turned the engine off. He extracted the keys and dangling the ring from the very tips of his right hand, he lifted the keys well above the level of the dashboard so there was no question his hand held no weapon. Keeping his left hand on the wheel, he passed the keys out of the driver's window and handed them to the police officer.

"Just keep your hands on the wheel, sir. This won't take long."

Hopkins kept both his hands on the wheel and smiled weakly at the SWAT trooper in front of the truck. Behind him the cargo doors of the truck were pulled open. The well-oiled back gate was opened and then quickly closed.

"You're quite right, sir. The truck is empty. Please step outside, sir. We still have to check the cab – and you."

"Am I under arrest?" Hopkins said it with such trepidation the SWAT trooper with the keys in his hand laughed.

"Should you be?"

"Well, I ran a few yellow lights getting here. I was afraid my evil ways had caught up with me. What's going on here?"

"You're not under arrest and as to what's going on here, I'm not so sure myself. All I do know is you're expected but I'm under strict orders to make sure nothing goes awry. So, if you will, I need to search you."

"Not a problem." Hopkins turned toward the side of the truck and leaned against it. He spread his feet and the policeman began patting him down. "If you find any money, let me know."

After the body search, Hopkins was directed to a side door in the garage.

Chapter 57

"Sounds like we're on our own people," The assistant branch manager said, his voice reverberating in the hallway no one could see. "Everybody find a wall and see if we can find a door somewhere."

There was a general shuffling of feet and the sound of hands fumbling in the dark. Greenleaf found a door handle but it was locked. Someone found a nonworking light switch and Cheri Molk found a working drinking fountain. "At least we can have a drink," quipped one of the tellers.

Finally someone found a door that would open. Navigating by the sound of her voice, Greenleaf moved toward the door. Guided by her hands, she passed from a narrow hallway into a massive, cool room. From the way the sound dissipated, it clearly had a high, vaulted ceiling.

"Feel your way around the walls carefully," the Assistant Branch Manager said. "See if you can find a light switch."

"I already have," someone said, "but it takes one of those special keys to get the lights on."

"Well, keep feeling your way around the walls, maybe something will turn up."

Greenleaf's hands hit something familiar about five feet above the floor level. Even without the power of sight she knew instantly what it was and, without a second thought, grabbed the lever and gave it a power jerk. In the next instant emergency lights exploded to life and the wail of a fire alarm reverberated throughout the room.

It took less than a second for every true San Franciscan to know where he or she was. For those who didn't know, the name of the room was written in six-inch letters running along the curved wall of the room: De Young Museum Planetarium.

Chapter 58

Hopkins was finally ushered into the garage by Chief Thayer.

"It's about time you got here." Harrah snapped when Douglas arrived. "You certainly took your time."

Hopkins was clearly at a loss as to what was going on. He looked from Harrah to Noonan to Chief Thayer and then back again, rubbing his wrists the whole time. There was a long, pregnant pause during which Hopkins did nothing, simply stood in the center of the garage in front of the pallet of $10 million with his mouth open. His appearance was so demented had he been drooling someone would have gone looking for a straitjacket. He started to say something but then thought better of it.

Harrah was leaning leisurely against one of the open studs in the garage and smoking a cigar. Noonan, with a cheery smile was leaning against a woodworking bench while the rest of the room stood in stony silence.

"I guess you're all wondering why I called you here." Hopkins finally gathered enough strength to make a weak attempt at humor.

"In a matter of speaking," grumbled Chief Thayer, "To be sure. Just for the record, Douglas, we need some answers and we need them now."

"Whatever I can do for you, Chief."

Harrah eased himself away from the wall and tapped his cigar elegantly with the forefinger of his right hand. Just as Chief Thayer started to speak, Harrah politely but forcefully jammed himself into the conversation. "Hopkins, will you please verify for the Chief this money," he indicated the pallet of $10,000 bricks, "is money belonging to English Petroleum."

"Certainly." Hopkins looked at the Chief; clearly happy he was being asked to answer a question to which there was no doubt. "Chief, this $10 million is the property of English Petroleum."

"No kidding?!" Chief Thayer showed mock surprise on his face. "I am shocked!"

"Yes, it is a surprise, Chief." Harrah spoke slowly as Hopkins regained his composure. "We at English Petroleum don't do things the way you Americans do, which is why we engage security professionals like Billingsley and Hardesty to back up your measures. We can't always depend on the American system or the police. Frankly, this entire episode has shown us we were correct in our assumption."

"Which is?" Thayer asked.

"We cannot depend on American security for our assets, Chief. Which is why we went to rather elaborate measures to safeguard our cash – which was legally registered with the IRS, let me assure you."

Chief Thayer shook his head sadly. "Just a second, Hopkins. I just want one answer from you. Did you or did you not arrange to have this $10 million placed here with the consent of English Petroleum?"

Hopkins started to speak but Harrah cut him off before the insurance agent could respond.

"Chief Thayer! Douglas Hopkins is in the employ of English Petroleum. As our insurance representative and security consultant, our instructions to him are confidential. You should know that. You should also appreciate our position. We do not flash around where and when we are moving large amounts of cash."

"So Mr. Hopkins was well aware of where this $10 million was all day yesterday? This is what you are telling us, correct?"

Noonan stepped forward and casually picked up some of the loose $100 bills from one of the bricks which had burst out of its paper wrapper. Noonan fanned the bills like they were a hand of cards in euchre as he looked at Harrah.

Harrah was not impressed. "What I am telling you is none of our instructions to Mr. Hopkins are your business. Besides, you're not with the San Francisco Police, Captain. You have no jurisdiction here."

"Yes, I see your point." Noonan tapped the bills into a single pile in his hand and bent them in the middle to form a long, narrow ruler-like bundle which he used as a pointer. "However, sir, I don't remember you

Chapter 58

saying anything of the sort when I was in your office yesterday. In fact, I remember you indicating your money was missing."

Harrah smiled blandly. "I don't actually remember what I did say, Captain. But I am sure I tried to keep the fate of the $10 million as quiet as possible. Mr. Hopkins was instructed to do the same."

"So Hopkins knew where the $10 million was all the time? Is this what you are telling us?" Thayer wrung his hands and stepped forward in anger. Harrah turned sideways to eye him directly.

"Chief Thayer, regardless of my respect for you personally and the uniform you wear, you have to understand I must answer to a higher authority: the home office. Their instructions are precise. I am to safeguard the assets of English Petroleum. Period. As you can see," he indicated the $10 million on the floor of the garage, "I have done the task admirably. The money was never stolen. It was never misplaced. It was just out of sight of the police and the assumption was naturally made the cash had been stolen."

"What about the other individuals who were here before the Chief arrived?" Detective Smith advanced on the pallet and put her foot up on the bricks.

"Other individuals? I don't know anything about them. I assume they were retained by Douglas Hopkins to add security. I don't know anything about them – except that they did a good job at protecting the assets of English Petroleum. I would appreciate it if you would take your foot off those money bricks, Detective. And Detective Noonan, would you please put all of those bills back where you found them. Once again, let me remind you all of these bills are the property of English Petroleum. Douglas! Will you please begin loading these bricks into the Ryder as we arranged?"

Hopkins, who had been standing mute during the entire confrontation, suddenly became animated. He started to move for the door but was stopped by Chief Thayer.

"Not so fast, Hopkins. We've got a long way to go before anyone walks away with $10 million. Now, Harrah, let me make sure I've got this correct." Chief Thayer faced Harrah. "You are saying this $10 million belongs to English Petroleum and it was never in the Fargo-Butterfield First even though it was listed there and it was never taken because it was never there."

"Correct. The insurance company, Mr. Hopkins, was aware of the situation. It was part of our security arrangements."

"That's not what you said in your office."

"As I remember, what I said in my office was the IRS knew of the existence of the $10 million in cash. I never said anything about the money not being in the bank."

"That's very close to an obstruction of justice charge."

"That I didn't answer a question the police didn't ask? Spare me, Chief."

"A court might look at it differently," continued Chief Thayer.

"Then why did he," indicating Hopkins, "lead us on a wild goose chase looking for the millions?"

"It wasn't a goose chase at all, Chief. Douglas Hopkins' instructions from us were to give every assistance to the San Francisco Police but the location of the $10 million was not to be disclosed."

"Which is still obstruction of justice, Harrah, a felony in this state." Smith was reaching for her handcuffs when Noonan stopped her.

"I'm sure those won't be necessary, Detective Smith." Noonan gave Chief Thayer a strange look. "I'm sure the Regional Vice President of Pacific Rim Operations for English Petroleum wouldn't lie to us and, to be honest, Detective, we never asked Mr. Hopkins directly if he knew where the $10 million was."

"Yes, but I . . ." Smith was not happy with this turn of events.

"Detective," Noonan shot Smith a harsh glance. She looked across the garage at Chief Thayer who was silent and expressionless. "We have no reason to believe – or proof – this money is not the $10 million owned by English Petroleum. While we may have our suspicions, we cannot be sure. Where English Petroleum chooses to safeguard their money is their concern, of course, and as long as their representative does not lie to us, well, we have no choice but to assume what they say is true."

"Thank you very much, Captain. I certainly underestimated you." Harrah's face broke into a wide grin.

"Yes, a Daniel come to Judgment, eh? I guess such would fit. Shakespeare was your contribution to world literature."

"An educated man." Harrah turned to Chief Thayer. "Chief, would it be acceptable if I loaded my company's assets now?"

Chief Thayer looked at Harrah, then at Noonan. There was silence for a moment and then Noonan jumped back into the fray.

"Well, Mr. Harrah. I am just a visitor here so the ultimate decision will have to be made by Chief Thayer, of course. Still, it would ease the tenseness of the situation if you would be so kind as to sign a statement here

Chapter 58

and now certify that these bills are the property of English Petroleum and you accept responsibility for them. You know, paperwork, just in case someone else says they lost $10 million over the last 24 hours."

Harrah laughed. "Certainly. You are a card, you are, Detective."

"Of course there is the matter of the other money English Petroleum had flown in this evening." Noonan gently rubbed his left cheek with his left hand. "If the police were to examine the shipping documentation from Federal Express and compare it to the money still in your immediate possession, the figures would match, correct?"

"Not exactly," Harrah didn't bat an eye. "There would be an $8 million discrepancy which we are handling administratively."

"I see," Noonan muttered. "But you are still assuring us the total $10 million here and the $10 million just flown into San Francisco are all accounted for?"

"Yes. There is no money missing."

Noonan smiled again. "Fine. Detective Smith, will you please fill out such a declaration in triplicate? One for the San Francisco Police, one for English Petroleum and one for your field report."

Smith was frozen in place. She looked at Chief Thayer who was thoughtful for a moment, a look on his face clearly showed he was confused. Then he nodded his head. Smith shrugged and pulled out her notepad. "Exactly what do you want this to say?" she asked Noonan.

"Oh, I don't know. How about, 'I, Regional Vice President Harrah of English Petroleum do hereby verify the $10 million at 1906 Ruef and the $10 million which was flown into San Francisco this evening and is at another location are the sole property of English Petroleum.' That should do it. Don't you think so, Mr. Harrah?"

"Sounds splendid to me." Harrah beamed like a Cheshire cat.

As Smith filled out the paperwork in triplicate, Harrah indicated Billingsley and Hardesty should begin gathering up all the loose bills and put them in the garbage bag on the top of the pallet. Hopkins jingled his keys and started to walk toward the garage door.

"I think I'll back the truck into the garage."

"A capital idea," Noonan said as he raised the garage door.

Chapter 59

Thayer shook his head in disbelief as he drove south on US. 101 heading for San Francisco International Airport. "Well, Heinz, I'm sorry we didn't do as well as we could. At least we got the hostages out safe and sound."

"But you have it all, George. We have all the clues you need to round up the rest of the gang."

"Really?"

"Sure. In fact, you're going to catch all the rats in the same trap this evening."

"How?"

"Well, let's look at how the robbery took place. Forget the safety deposit boxes. Their robbery was just a ruse. In fact, when you finally look at the real numbers I think you'll find there really wasn't that much worth stealing in the boxes at all."

"Why not?"

"Because safety deposit boxes are used by people in the area to store their valuables. Look at the area where the Butterfield-Fargo First was located."

"So?"

"I looked over the neighborhood. The only kind of customers the bank would have had were ones with both hands out – and full of pistols. Not exactly a high rent district. In fact, you might even wonder why the bank opened up a branch there."

"I think it was part of a Re-Vitalize the Inner City, the RIC program, by the Chamber of Commerce."

"Yeah. So Butterfield-Fargo puts in a small bank. Depressed neighborhood. It was their excuse to meet FDIC guidelines on offering money to poor neighborhoods. Which is the reason the bank didn't gripe very loudly when Hopkins began running cash through their office. They didn't have a strong portfolio because of the neighborhood but the millions in cash made them look very good. Which is also why Hopkins had such a run of the operation. He was making the bank look good on paper. But it didn't change the fact the neighborhood didn't have anything to put in the safety deposit boxes."

"So there wasn't anything in the safety deposit boxes?"

"Probably not much. The perps hit the bank because the $10 million was there. Rather, it wasn't there. It never made it into the bank. Hopkins set the whole thing up to look like a robbery to cover the fact the $10 million had never been deposited."

"But can you prove that?"

"I don't need to. Let me explain. After the perps took whatever they could find in the safety deposit boxes, they took off with the hostages."

"Yeah, I know. I was there, remember?"

"Yes. But your disadvantage was you had to follow the crime in real-time, so to speak. Second-by-second you followed the perps while they, on the other hand, had their actions planned out months in advance. They were just waiting for the right night, a night with heavy fog to cover the disappearance of the bus on the Golden Gate Bridge. You did everything they expected you to do. While they were weaving through the streets of San Francisco, you thought they were lost. In fact, they were setting you up."

"However they did it, it was a good job."

"Not really. It was very simple. You thought the bus went out onto the bridge and that's the way you played it. In fact, the bus with the hostages simply drove away. Your men were fooled by a cellular phone call."

"How?"

"You believed the man on the cellular phone was on the bus. In fact, he was not. He knew what was happening on the basis of timing. While he was yelling at you to stay away from the bus, which wasn't heading for the bridge, his men – probably one man – was setting up the diversion on the bridge in motion. What the perps needed was time, less than a handful of seconds, time to get out of the area and make the switch from the Greyhound to the police vehicle you found in Hunter's Point. The hostages had to be on their way to the Hunter's Point Salvage Yard before a dragnet went up. After all, the safest place to be when the police are looking for you is at a police station, right?"

"Yeah. Go on."

"Well, the hostages were taken to the Hunter's Point Salvage Yard and the bus was driven back to the Greyhound terminal. The perps know what the San Francisco police were doing because they had an inside man. And a highly placed one. You knew that, Chief. Which is one of the reasons you sent for me."

"How did you know? And when?"

"Frankly I figured there was an inside man the moment I stepped off the airplane."

"It was just a good guess. How did you really know?"

"The minute I got off the plane I was approached by someone who wanted me to sign my book. The man was waiting in the right boarding area to catch me as I went by."

"So?"

"No one but the San Francisco Police knew I was coming to town. You told me that when you picked me up. It had to be an inside leak. There were so few people at police headquarters who were privy to what was going on you had to pick me up yourself."

"How did you know it wasn't a policeman at the airport?"

"I didn't. Not then. I just thought it was strange someone should have my book and be waiting in the boarding area when my plane landed. I didn't even know I was coming to San Francisco until just before the airliner left Seattle."

"It could have been someone who just happened to be in the airport. He might have bought the book in one of the bookstores at San Francisco International and spotted you while he was waiting for another plane."

"No. I checked. My book wasn't being sold in the airport. I also looked at the Arrivals/Departures to see if the man had been waiting for an outgoing flight. The next flight out of the boarding area was two hours later. No, he was waiting for me."

"So what if he was?"

"He wasn't just waiting for me, George. He had an accomplice. Remember, it was a warm day and I wasn't wearing the jacket?" The Chief nodded and Noonan continued. "My jacket was over my arm. While I was juggling my jacket to sign my book, the accomplice slipped a homing device into my jacket pocket."

Chapter 59

"That's quite a supposition even for you, Heinz."

"No, not really. You see, while I was out on the Golden Gate Bridge I came to the conclusion one of the critical features of this case was homing devices. Ergo, the inside man at the San Francisco Police Department had to be associated with tracking devices. In San Francisco, this meant Property."

"Still a stretch, Heinz."

"It wasn't until I had Detective Smith check out the bug which I found in my pocket with the equipment we had just bought. It looked just like a small camera battery but it was a bug. Smith checked it with a detector we bought downtown."

"Ah, a homing device?"

"A pretty sophisticated little puppy as it turns out. If I had come across it in my pocket by accident I would not have thought it was a homing device. It looked like a camera battery and I would have kept it thinking it had come from a dictating machine or some other piece of electronic equipment I had been using recently in Sandersonville. It was what the perps expected and it almost happened."

"So you knew you were bugged? Why would anyone want to bug you?"

"To know where I was all the time. It's pretty well known I wear my leather jacket most of the time. It's cold and wet in San Francisco most of the time. Thus I had to be wearing this jacket most of the time so what better place to put in a bug?"

"When did you know for sure?"

"When Smith and I were followed on my way to the Hunter's Point Salvage Yard. The minute we started moving south, we picked up a tail. We lost them and then we were ambushed near the salvage yard. As soon as I started south, the perps knew I was onto their first hideout."

"So you ditched the jacket."

"Yes, I did. Remember I sent it with you to have a button replaced and then have the jacket sent back to the hotel."

"Right. So the perps thought you were at the hotel."

"I'm sure they were in touch with the homing device person at the Police Department on a frequent basis. As long as they thought I was at the tailor in Chinatown or at the hotel, I was out of their hair."

"Very clever."

"Maybe. It gave me time to move around undetected so Smith and I could tail Hopkins. It was a hunch but it paid off."

The Chief started to ask a question and then remembered something to mention to Noonan. "By the way, we found the vehicle which was probably used to transport the hostages. It was a police truck with ten seats bolted to the inside of its cargo hold. Unfortunately it was found being trashed in Hunter's Point. A search of the back revealed another Butterfield-Fargo First deposit slip. The vehicle was taken to the Hunter's Point Salvage Yard where it was put under active guard until the lab team was through with the warehouse. The plates on the truck were traced to a junkyard in Sonoma where the original truck was still lying in state, a fact confirmed by the Sonoma Police. The vehicle registration was traced to a shipping company in New Jersey. There the trail ended. The vehicle had been sold at auction the previous year. The buyer had paid cash and left a phony name and address."

"I kind of figured it would be something along those lines."

Chief Thayer then snapped back on track. "But how did you get from Hopkins to the house on Ruef Street?"

"I followed the man who met Hopkins. Except it took a little doing. We had to fool him. So we used two vehicles. One to attract his attention."

"The purple Subaru!"

"Right. Not very subtle but enough to grab his attention. We wanted him to know he was being followed. When he lost Detective Smith, he figured he was in the clear."

"Then you got on the cell phone to Smith and she caught up with you."

"Right. Which reminds me, Chief. Detective Smith left the purple Subaru near the corner of Balboa and 25th. I'm sure Smith has had it picked up, but, just in case . . ."

"I'll send someone to check."

Chief Thayer pulled the car into a No Parking Zone in front of baggage claim. "Rank has its privileges," Thayer said as he smiled mischievously.

"Haven't I been here before?" Noonan pointed at the No Parking Zone sign. Thayer smiled and hit the flashing lights.

"I'm impressed. Turn 'em off."

Chief Thayer snapped off the flashing bubble gums but left the parking lights throbbing red and white. They fought their way through the crowd and into the hallway leading to the Alaska Airlines courtesy lounge. Once inside, Noonan picked up his jacket. He and Thayer then moved down the hallway toward the boarding area. It was a beautiful Sandersonville-like evening outside, lots of rain and cold wind.

Chief Thayer was walking leisurely while Noonan was putting on his jacket. "Now. You made it 1906 Ruef by tailing the man who met with Hopkins. How did you make the connection with English Petroleum?"

"Rasperson did. He went to English Petroleum and stumbled into Hopkins and the two thugs Harrah keeps around. He put two and two together and got four. Smart guy. We ran into him at 1906 Ruef staking out the place. Then he worked with us."

"I didn't see him at 1906 Ruef when I got there. Did he go back to the *Business Herald*?"

"Well, I don't know, George. They've got a paper coming out tomorrow morning. We'll just have to see what shows up on the front page."

Noonan plunged his hand into his pocket. He withdrew a small, coin-like object. He showed it to the Chief who had to put on his reading glasses to examine it properly.

"So this is what those high-tech homing devices look like," Chief Thayer said with interest. "Too bad it can't tell us where the perps are." The Chief handed the device back to Noonan who dropped it in his pocket.

"Well, it can't tell you but I think I can. While I was out on the Golden Gate Bridge I was faced with two problems. One was how the Greyhound bus disappeared. The other was what happened to the man who pulled the vanishing act."

"Don't you mean men? There were three bungee cords; therefore there must have been three men."

"No. One man. Once again, George, you're slipping into the trap the perps left for you. All together there weren't more than eight perps plus Hopkins and your inside man at the department. That makes four in the bank and four outside. What made it seem like more was they had cell phones."

"OK. How did the bus disappear?"

"It didn't. Here's what I'm guessing happened. Once the perps left the bank they dashed all over San Francisco with the cops on their tail."

"Right. Yelling all the way."

"Right. But the guy on the phone wasn't on the bus. You thought you were talking to a perp on the bus but, in fact, he was somewhere else, probably overlooking the Golden Gate Bridge. His job was to confuse you and he did his job well."

"But we saw the bus disappear!"

"No you didn't. What your men saw was a bus running without lights entering the General Douglas MacArthur Tunnel and heard a perp on your cell phone yelling about the bus being designed to fail. He yelled it was smoking and you broadcast the smoking to your men on the street."

"Correct."

"Well, what actually happened was a motorcycle with a smoke machine, the kind you could get from a movie set, drove inside the tunnel. The perp on the motorcycle was smoking the tunnel up while the bus was running toward the tunnel. The minute the Greyhound entered the tunnel, it braked fast and all the time the perp kept yelling about the smoke and you kept relaying the smoking information to your men."

"Then?" Thayer leaned forward expectantly.

"The motorcycle blasted out of the tunnel with the smoke machine billowing massive clouds behind him. He only had to go about a mile before he entered the bridge. Right behind him in the smoke the bus running without lights took a right turn onto Highway 101. Logic told your men to follow the smoke and they did. Which is exactly what the perps wanted them to do. While you followed the billowing smoke out onto the bridge, the Greyhound turned onto US 101 and made a beeline for a transfer point somewhere near the Greyhound yard. You assumed the bus was going onto the bridge because the smoke was leading you that way. When the bus made the Greyhound yard, the hostages came off and were loaded into a police bus. Then one of the perps parked the Greyhound against a building where buses are stored and switched plates. Then he walked away. End of story."

"But the helicopter followed the bus out onto the bridge!"

"Followed what? It was pea soup all night. The perps chose well. At best the helicopter saw a moving trail of smoke heading for the bridge. The minute the smoking passed Highway 101 it had no other option but to get out onto the bridge. Then the helicopter broke off the chase. It reported the vehicle was headed for the bridge."

"But the homing device on the bus was followed out onto the bridge!"

"That stumped me for a while. I knew the Greyhound hadn't gone onto the bridge but the homing device said it had. Which left me two options. The homing device had been switched from the Greyhound to the motorcycle, which was possible but unlikely, or the person tracking the homing device was lying. Since there was only one command center I assumed whoever was watching the computerized homing screen was the inside

Chapter 59

man. The homing device on the Greyhound was beeping correctly; the inside man just said it had gone out onto the bridge. The police believed the smoking vehicle in front of them was a bus so they followed it. The helicopter could not see anything because of the fog. When the command center said that the homing device placed the Greyhound on the bridge, who was going to dispute them?"

"But something went onto the bridge. Why didn't the cameras pick it up?"

"Good question. The vehicle was close enough to the cameras they should have picked up something even if the fog was thick. The logical answer is the video machines were tampered with. Someone recorded a calm night's activity and then fed it back into the camera's track. They only needed about three minutes to pull off the disappearing act. I'll bet someone, possibly a phony police officer or bridge inspector, gave a snap inspection a couple of days before the bank job. No one would have suspected anything was awry. After all, why worry about someone inspecting cameras when they haven't recorded anything? Then it was just a matter of following the cables and clamping into the leads under the control shed. There's not a lot of security on the bridge because it's not needed. It made the tampering easy."

"But we would have discovered the tampering eventually."

"So what? These perps figured to make their getaway with $10 million. No one gets hurt, there's no extradition. What they needed was time. So what if you found the video recorder two days later? So what if you had enough evidence to fire the inside man at the department in two days? So what if Hopkins was under suspicion two days later? Everyone would be out of the country. As long as no one got killed it would be almost impossible to get them back for trial."

Noonan took a breath and then continued. "But, if you don't find some kind of electronic doodads under the control shed, look at the lines very carefully. I'm sure you'll find indications of clamp marks. For all I know those new clamp systems might have remote control releases. If the perps got themselves a good radio-controlled system they could have hit a button and, splash, the whole mechanism falls 200 feet to the water and sinks another 200 to bedrock. I'll bet the current is so strong on the bottom any piece of machinery was rolled to a ball before it made it into the Pacific."

"This is all confusing, Heinz. But what about the three bungee cords?"

"Good question. Those three cords were placed there for a number of good reasons. First, the perps wanted you to believe they had gotten off the bridge where the bungees were found. It was on the city side of the bridge – where they wanted you to look for clues. It worked. You assumed the men had left the bridge by bouncing down to a boat. Three bungee cords, three men. It also screwed up your count of the number of perps. Since you believed the perps got off on the city side of the bridge, you began searching for clues on the San Francisco waterfront."

"Yeah."

"Once again, it's what the perps wanted you to think. The cords had actually been placed there the previous night, possibly by the same man who did the inspection of the control shed. No one was going to ask him what he was doing; he was a cop or an inspector. But the bungee cords weren't noticed because there was no reason to look for them. They were installed to mislead you. What actually happened is the smoking vehicle scooted past the three cords and went another half mile to where I had photographs taken."

"Go on."

"Which is where the motorcycle stopped. The bridge was closed off by this time so there wasn't any danger of oncoming traffic, vehicular or pedestrian. The man on the motorcycle simply scaled the fence and attached a pulley to the descending cable at the location – if there wasn't another cable already there. He pulleyed the motorcycle up over the fence and dropped it onto the Pacific Ocean side of the bridge. The police would never find it because they would be looking for a Greyhound bus, not a motorcycle and besides, it was on the wrong side of the bridge. After the motorcycle went, the smoke machine went."

"Which is what damaged the section of fence you photographed."

"Yeah. I think so. We'll probably never know for sure."

"OK. So far everything you've said is possible. How does the man leave the bridge without being spotted?"

"You know, George, that was the toughest part of this case. I could not figure out how the man got away. The bridge was closed off from both sides; there was a helicopter in the air and men watching the bridge. He couldn't walk off, he couldn't drop off, and he couldn't climb up into the bridge. If he had left the bridge any of those ways he would have been discovered. So he had to fly out."

"Fly!"

"Yup, fly. It was his only option. He had to fly. But he couldn't fly toward the city. He had to fly out to sea."

Chapter 59

Chief Thayer shook his head in amazement. Then he laughed with amusement and turned around in his chair to look Noonan in the eye. "You almost had me fooled there, Heinz. He flew out! Ha! Classic! Even if he could fly off the bridge with a hang glider, he's heading out into the jet black Pacific Ocean. How's he going to find someone to pick him up? If there's any one thing the chopper could have seen was a light in the jet black Pacific."

"Everything you've said is true, George. Which is why he went over the side in a hang glider. He had to get away from the bridge, away from where he would be spotted. It wouldn't really have been difficult. The same inspector who put the bungee cords on the bridge stashed the glider earlier, probably. Once the motorcycle went over the side, the man left in a hang glider going in the one direction no one would have expected him to go."

"OK! OK!" George laughed heartily. "Let's just say he did fly away. But you don't live around here. Those currents out there are treacherous. He's out there in the jet black of the Pacific. There is nothing out there. Nothing. Even if he does make it out into the nothingness, how is anyone going to find him? I've been out there on a calm day and couldn't see people in the water right in front of me."

"It had me stumped too. I thought about it and suddenly realized your inside man was a critical component of the robbery. Not only did he lie about where the bus was headed and track me all day, he also brought the boat and the hang glider together."

"How?"

"The same way he tracked me. With homing devices. All he needed to do was get the hang glider and the boatsman close. He could do it on a computer screen. You know, tell the boatsman to move 200 yards to the left or right."

"How'd he pass along the information? Shout?"

"No, George. The same way we kept off the police channel. With a cellular phone. He used a cellular phone. No one could trace the call. He was in touch with the boatsman and guided him close. Then it was a matter of using a night scope. If the man in the water had some kind of a red light he wouldn't be hard to spot. They had all night. No one was expecting to look out to sea to spot the perps so they had a free hand."

Chief Thayer was silent for a moment, mulling over the idea. "But then they'll have to go somewhere. They can't come back into the bay. Where did they go?"

"I'm betting they went north. To Bodega Bay."

"Quite a jump, Heinz. There are a lot of docks and coves between here and Bodega Bay. Why that particular place?"

"Let's just call it a hunch."

"Based on what?"

"Well, when I was talking to Hopkins, he said he had a boat which he moored in Bodega Bay. He said he had named it the Cagliostro, after the alchemist."

"Never heard of him."

"Most people haven't either. Which is why Hopkins named his boat the Cagliostro. He's an 18th-century figure. But he was more than an alchemist as Hopkins claimed. He was also a chiseler, clairvoyant and charlatan, exactly the kind of a man who would think he could mastermind a multi-million dollar heist. Ironically, he's also associated with a scam which was certainly the beginning of the end of the King of France, Louis XVI and his wife, Marie Antoinette."

Chief Thayer looked at Noonan with astonishment. "You really do know your European history. Maybe, if history repeats itself, Hopkins will be the beginning of the fall of our august vice president of Pacific Rim Operations."

"At the very least he's going to cause Harrah a lot of explaining."

Thayer shook his head. "So you think those men are on the Cagliostro in Bodega Bay?"

"It's as good a bet as any. I'd also say they're having a heck of a fight. Remember when Hopkins showed up at the Ruef Street address late?"

"Yeah."

"He was late because he was doing some freelancing. Your people reported he had gone to the first warehouse and picked up three crates."

"Uh-huh."

"Those crates were full of cash. Hopkins was picking up his cash first, making sure he was getting his. It's not going to make anyone else very happy, particularly when Hopkins doesn't show up."

"Wait here and I'll send a squad car to..."

Noonan put his hand on the Chief's arm. "Chief, don't worry. It's taken care of. While you were addressing the press outside your office, I took the liberty of calling the FBI and they're handling the matter. They're so good at claiming all the credit I figured it was only fair they do a little quality work on the case."

"You told them while I was addressing the press?"

"And what a masterful job you were doing too, George. I was envious. And I was also pleased you didn't mention my name. It's so hard to take vacations with so many robberies about."

Both men laughed.

"How about Hopkins?"

"If he's smart he's here at the airport flying out. He's got his million, all legal, so there's nothing you can do about him. If the five or six perps are still in Bodega Bay, you can snatch them. They're still guilty of bank robbery and kidnapping. Unless they rat on Hopkins, he's in the clear."

"So Hopkins slides?"

"No, none of them do. Don't worry about him. He had to cut some deals with the underworld to pull off a $10 million deal. What do you think is going to happen if he escapes with $1 million and everyone else in the caper gets caught? He can never come back here. He'll be lucky to stay alive. Regardless of what Harrah said, I doubt a company as large as English Petroleum is going to let a two-bit insurance man hustle them out of $10 million."

"Do you think this was all Hopkins' idea?"

The Chief shook his head sadly.

"He was probably the one setting up the San Francisco end of the operation. He knew the owners of 1906 Ruef were going to be out of town because the painters and contractors were probably part of his laundering operation. This gave him a base of operations. But there were barely enough people in his band to cover all the bases."

"How do you know?"

"When Rasperson got into the van he said he had only seen four people since he had gotten into the bushes. He was concerned he would be spotted so he played like the Vietnam vet he was. He blended into the environment. But all he saw were people in and around the garage. No one appeared to be watching the road for suspicious characters. This told me the perps either didn't have enough people to cover all the angles or felt the hostages were an ace they could use at any time. I now think both were correct. In the long run, it didn't matter."

"You are a sly one, you are, Heinz Noonan."

"Not really, George. Just very lucky. And if my luck still holds, I'll be able to make it to Anchorage before my father-in-law uses my fly-in king salmon reservations."

"Best of luck, Heinz."

Noonan started to walk toward the boarding tunnel when he suddenly stopped and scratched his head Columbo-style. Chief Thayer looked at Noonan with a strange expression. Noonan smiled and patted the Chief on the back. "George, I just remembered I need you to do something for me."

"What are you not telling me, Heinz?" Chief Thayer gave a strange what-is-it-now smile.

"Oh, just a little thing. Remember you said there was nothing we could do about English Petroleum?"

"Yeah. They played me like a fiddle. It's just too bad we can't get them on something."

"Who knows?" Noonan had a strange smile on his face as he leaned against an insurance machine. "George, I seem to have made a mistake back there in the garage."

"Oh?"

Noonan dug an envelope out of his pants pocket and handed it to Chief Thayer. The Chief opened the envelope and, with surprise etched on his face, looked at a spread of $100 bills.

"It seems while I was examining some of the $100 bills in the collection English Petroleum claimed was theirs some of the bills accidentally went up my sleeve. It was a terrible indiscretion on my part. I'm sure they'll miss the bills. Will you make sure they get these back?"

"Just happened to slip up your sleeve? Uh-huh. You mean you palmed these bills."

"George! Palming someone else's property would have been illegal. An innocent error, I assure you. Now I am rectifying any error. I'm returning these suddenly-discovered bills with apologies. You will see these bills are returned? I'm sure that English Petroleum will find that they are missing."

"Right, Heinz. I know you. Now, what do you have up your sleeve – other than the bills you just gave me?"

"George, what makes you think I've planned some underhanded scheme?"

"Heinz!"

Noonan looked at the ceiling of the courtesy lounge. "While I was in your office I took the liberty of photocopying those $100 bills." He pointed of the bills Chief Thayer held in his hand.

"Yeah."

"And I put the copies in an envelope with a copy of the property transfer from English Petroleum. You know, the one signed by Harrah stating the $20 million in San Francisco was his?"

"I'm with you so far."

"Well, I have to admit it, George. While you were talking to the press I also stole an envelope from your desk and about a dollar's worth of stamps. Then I dropped the photocopies in the mail for Rasperson. I'm sure he'll know what to do with them."

"Clue me in. What will he do with them?"

"Well, we can't get English Petroleum. They said the $20 million was their property and you couldn't prove them wrong. Hopkins confirmed their claim. End of story. Right?"

"Yeah."

"But we know differently. The original $10 million was at the center of a robbery and the other $10 million was exchange money. We can't prove it, of course, even though we know it."

"Win some, lose some."

"But Rasperson could call the IRS and trace these bills. And when he gets a hold of some photocopies of the $100 bills which will be found with the perps the FBI is probably arresting right now in Bodega Bay...."

Thayer smiled. "He'll have solid proof where those bills came from. We can't get English Petroleum but the IRS can! Good thinking. You know," he looked at Noonan mischievously, "I'm sure someone will be able to get him a raft of photocopies of investigation documents when those perps are arrested."

Noonan smiled. "I kind of thought so. We can't report anything because we don't have anything to report. No theft means all the documents are public information. And Rasperson, well, you know how rude those press people can be."

Noonan turned to go and then reached into his jacket pocket. He brought out a small, flat item looking much like a camera battery. "Here, a little memento from my day here in San Francisco. It's just like a dog, George." Noonan smiled. "It'll follow you anywhere."

Made in the USA
Columbia, SC
13 October 2024